WOLF HUNTED

FORTITUDE WOLVES - BOOK THREE

NICOLE R. TAYLOR

CHAPTER 1

SLOANE

The sun was hot on my shoulders, the rays frying my skin to a crisp.

Pressing my fingers on the arms of my aviator sunglasses behind my ears, I angled them up so I could look at the horizon without the polarised filter. There was a hazy brown smudge breaking up the expanse of blue.

Bushfires.

I'd had enough of the sweltering heat of burning buildings and was glad we were in the Mallee—the hot, dry, flat plains of northwest Victoria—away from all that. Not that it was cooler...it was just a different kind of summer this close to the outback.

I allowed my sunglasses to fall back into place, and I rubbed my eyes, forcibly trying to remove the images of flames roaring towards the sky. The inferno had taken hold of DeLuca's remote miner's cottage so easily, the smoke and stench blotting out the stars. The whole thing had been an unbelievable sight—I'd never seen anything like it before.

The roof of the motel was empty, the high heat keeping most people away from the lacklustre patio area. Broken and faded lawn chairs were scattered across the tarred surface behind me, and tattered beach umbrellas cast mediocre shade. At some point, someone had the foresight to blow up an inflatable wading pool, but it had long since burst from neglect. Chaser sure knew how to find the shittiest hole this side of a bush oasis.

My feet dangled over the side of the building, my backside firmly behind the lip of the flimsy railing my arms were threaded through. Staring at my boots, I closed one eye then the other, focusing on the car park below. The right toe had a deep gouge mark across the leather that hadn't been there two nights ago.

A gust of wind stirred my hair and a tumbleweed bounced across the street. *The wind is whipping up*, I thought. *Sucks for those bushfires.*

There were lots of things I should've been thinking about, but I couldn't focus. It wasn't the heat or my exhaustion, it was just...trauma, I guessed. Ever since I'd woken up in the motel room downstairs, I hadn't closed my eyes. I couldn't.

Reaching into the pocket of my jean shorts, I pulled out the engagement ring I'd stolen from

Marini's bedside table back at the Fortitude compound.

My fingers worried the gold band, and my fingernail dragged along the ridges of the diamond setting. It was the only thing I had from my mother, and before the other day, I'd had nothing at all. I didn't like what it stood for, but it was hers, which was all that mattered. *Daddy gave that to me on the beach*, she'd said. I hated that he'd kept it.

"All right?"

Closing my fist around the ring, I glanced up at Chaser. It always amazed me how he could walk in the sun. As a vampire, he should technically burst into flames at the slightest hint of UV, but a spell cast by a witch gave him the shield he needed—and another had bound him into slavery that'd lasted a century.

"I've got a headache," I replied, leaning my head against the railing.

"You should drink more water." He sat beside me and wiped the back of his arm across his brow. "You should put ice on your neck. It's the perfect weather for it."

I shrugged and glanced at the horizon.

"There's bushfires near the border," he said after a moment.

I didn't like the mention of fire. We still hadn't heard from Gasket, who Chaser said had ridden off with the rest of the Fortitude Wolves to hunt down the remaining renegades after the standoff at the cottage.

That was two nights ago.

"I don't like it," I murmured. "It's too open."

"We're safe here," Chaser said. "I made sure of it."

I grunted, turning my head so I was staring at the scrub. The wolf inside me still buzzed with the memory of my kill, the unexplored part of my psyche a little terrifying. It bayed for more, but this time, it wanted the blood of the immortal.

On the one hand, I wanted to run in the other direction, the thought of more heartache and pain too much to handle. On the other, nothing would be as satisfying as murdering King, the head honcho of the vampires who believed I was their ticket to true immortality. The man my father was going to sell me to as a loaded weapon, to die in a ritual that bound their entire bloodline. He was also the man who was responsible for killing Chaser's wife and turning him into a vampire—otherwise known as the whole psychotic package.

I had promised revenge and freedom for the both of us, and it was far too late to turn back now.

"Sloane?"

"We should be planning, not sitting in a musty motel room," I said, unable to hold on to my annoyance a second longer. "Can you get a respiratory disease from mould? Because I feel like I'm getting one."

Chaser gave me his trademark blank look. He was a master at hiding his emotions, which mainly annoyed me but must have been a riot when he was out on a job. Until recently, he'd been my late father's vampire slave. An image of Marini's vacant eyes appeared in my mind, and I shook my head. Chaser was bound by a magical talisman, so he had to follow the alpha's orders, but he could only bear it because he'd turned his back on his humanity. Luckily for him, I now had control of the talisman after Gasket had given it up.

If things had just gone the way they were supposed to, I'd have an entire werewolf pack riding into battle behind me, but the coup had been screwed before it had even gone down, and now I was in hiding with Chaser. The two of us against a supernatural vampire organisation that had its claws sunk into every major law enforcement agency. I may as well fling myself off the side of this shitty motel right now and be done with it.

"You are not alone," Chaser said, reading my mind with uncanny accuracy.

"What? Are you a psychic now?"

"Having the plan go off without a hitch was a dream, Sloane," he replied. "They know we're in hiding, planning something, so we may as well take our time."

Take our time? I wanted to scream into the void until my brain exploded. It'd only been three months. My whole life had been a joke. Thinking about my unfinished online university degree, everything seemed an epic waste of time.

"I don't want to live like this," I muttered, my heart sinking.

"Neither do I," Chaser agreed. "That's why we have to plan better this time. We went into Fortitude grossly unprepared."

I grunted, not wanting to acknowledge that he was right.

"We had passion but lacked proper strategy."

"We winged it," I said.

Chaser nodded. "This time, we figure it out. The Hollow Men aren't Fortitude."

"No, they aren't."

"Besides..." he trailed off, his brow creasing. Plucking his sunglasses from his shirt pocket, he slid them on and gazed out at the horizon.

"Besides, what?" I asked, lifting my head.

He shrugged, folding his arms on top of the railing. "*Chaser.*"

"Besides..." He sighed, then tilted his head towards me. "You haven't talked about what happened."

"I don't need to talk about what happened." I scowled, any ease our conversation had instilled in my heart evaporating. "It's in the past."

"Sloane, you mauled your father to death."

"Glad to see you describe it so tactfully," I drawled, wriggling away from the edge of the roof. Rising to my feet, I brushed my palms over my backside, dusting off the grit from the flaky, tarred surface.

"Sloane," Chaser exclaimed, standing. He grabbed

my arm and pulled, yanking me around. "You have to face it at some point, and I'd rather it wasn't with a gun in your hand."

"*Let me go.*" I wrenched myself free. "I don't need to face anything. I knew who he was, Chaser, and I damn well know the world is a better place without him in it. He's not the first man I killed, remember? There was the vampire who tried to kill you on the side of the road. I shot him and it did nothing to my mental wellbeing."

"Sloane...you collapsed. You turned so fast, it was unnatural."

"So?" I scoffed and gestured at him. "I'm the wolf who can turn whenever she wants. Screw the moon! What about you? I hardly know anything about you, and I have these...*feelings*. I'd go so far as to say the L-word, but how can I when I don't know—" I let out a frustrated cry.

"Don't turn this back on me. I'm trying to help you."

"Maybe I'm just that indifferent about it," I said, knowing it was a lie. I hadn't slept a wink because I was afraid of what my dreams would reveal.

Chaser pursed his lips. "I know we haven't had time," he said after a moment's silence. "I know there are things you don't know about my past, but know this... I'm standing here as a free man because of *you*. I'm no longer indentured to Fortitude; I no longer have to kill on command. And I sure as hell don't have to answer to anyone I don't want to. *You* gave me that, Sloane."

"The talisman still binds you, Chaser."

"And you're the one who possesses it."

I shook my head. "But you won't be truly free until we can break the spell."

"It's close enough for now."

I didn't agree, but there were too many spinning plates in the air. If someone managed to take the talisman from me, they'd have control of him...and he wouldn't be able to say no. If the Hollow Men found out about it, then we were both screwed.

"So I have all the power," I said, jutting out my chin. "I could make you shut up, you know."

"You wouldn't dare," he murmured. "And I won't help you further your denial."

I tensed, steeling myself to shout at him again, but he fisted his hands in my hair and pulled me close, his lips crushing mine, then he tore away with a gasp etched with longing.

"You want to believe in something?" he murmured, his breath hot against my skin. "Something good?" His body curved as if he was sheltering me from the world. "Then believe in us."

"Chaser..."

"I only just started," he whispered. "Don't leave me now."

I rubbed my palms over his chest, feeling the coldness of his body underneath the fabric of his shirt.

I explored my way upwards until my hands circled his neck. They were far too small to close the entire way around, but I felt the thrumming of his pulse all the same.

He had a vulnerable glint in his eyes, and Chaser was never vulnerable. That was how I knew he was telling the truth. He believed I needed to grieve my murderous, psychotic father while I believed I should've torn out his throat sooner. The point was, Chaser was right. This time, we needed to plot. The Hollow Men were vampires, some of them hundreds of years old.

"Fine," I said. "We do it your way. We plan."

His eyes narrowed.

"And don't you dare talk to me about him again," I added, my lip curling. "I hope they left him out in the sun to rot."

Chaser nodded and glanced at the sky. "Either way, *you* need to get out of the sun."

"I hope that wasn't a metaphor because I'm all out of patience for thinly veiled attacks on my personal decisions."

"Dehydration is known to turn people into raging bitches," he said with a smirk.

I rolled my eyes and let his neck go before I actually throttled him. Backing away, I screwed up my face. "Are you coming?" I asked, beckoning Chaser to follow. "There's no time to waste. We've got to start planning our forever, you know."

CHAPTER 2

SLOANE

The revolver was sitting on the table when I stepped into the motel room.

The mother-of-pearl grip shimmered in the light, and I shivered despite the heat. I didn't know why Chaser brought it with us. The gun symbolised everything Fortitude had been under my father, and I wasn't entirely sure I wanted to keep it.

"You haven't heard from Gasket?" I asked, sitting on the end of the bed.

"No. It's only a matter of time," he replied, filling a glass with water from the bathroom sink.

"Is that safe to drink?" I grimaced as Chaser handed me the glass. Lifting it to the light, I checked for floaties. "I heard there was lead in the water out here. You know, from all the industrial mining they did out here back in the day."

"Seriously? That's what you're worried about?"

"Lead poisoning is no laughing matter."

Chaser raised an eyebrow and fished around in the plastic bag hanging off the corner of one of the chairs. After a moment of annoying crinkling, he tossed me a packet of ibuprofen. "Here, take some for your headache."

"I'm a werewolf who can supernaturally heal. I don't need headache tablets."

"You can, but you're not immune to everything," Chaser told me. "You are a wolf, but you're mortal.... Just take the damn pills, Sloane."

Shrugging, I slipped two tablets into my mouth and chased them down with some water. Seriously, worse things had happened to me, so what was a little lead? I rubbed my temple as the mattress dipped and Chaser sat beside me.

He took the sheet of pills from my hand and set it onto the bedside table.

"Are you okay?" I asked, realising I hadn't asked. I didn't think I had to, but every day held a new surprise for us.

"I'm fine."

"I haven't seen you...*eat*."

His gaze lowered. "I took care of it."

"You...?" I tensed. I still don't know what it meant for a vampire to 'feed'. He'd taken some blood from me before, but I knew he was being careful then.

"I don't kill people," he said, reading my expression. "Afterwards, I heal the wound, then make them forget. I have my humanity now. I wouldn't…"

"I didn't mean…" I hesitated. "Chaser, I'm just trying to understand."

"I don't like talking about it." He was silent for a moment, then added, "When I first turned, it was difficult. I couldn't control what I'd become. There were…*accidents*." He grimaced. "But I can control it now. You don't have to worry."

I said nothing, I just placed my hand on his back and soothed my palm in a slow circle. He'd never told me how he'd turned, just that it wasn't pretty. The fact that he was opening up at all was more than enough for me.

A shrill ring pierced the silence.

"You better answer it," I said.

Chaser picked up the phone and checked the screen. "It's Gasket." He answered the call, put it on speaker, and then set it on the bed.

"Gasket," I said. "You've got news?"

"Hey, Sloane. You okay?"

"I'm fine. What's going on there? Have you found the renegades yet?"

"We lost them on the road," he explained, and Chaser cursed under his breath. The last thing we needed was to worry about two separate enemies coming after us.

"And the house?" Chaser asked. "How many of ours made it out?"

"Forty," Gasket replied. "We lost eight guys in the firefight."

I glanced at Chaser, but his reaction was zero, as per usual. Eight good guys were now in the ground, casualties of our messed-up coup.

"The renegades?" he asked. "How many are left?"

"Hard to say. Thirty... Thirty-five."

"What about Shondra, Kelly, and the others?" I chipped in.

"They're safe, Sloane," Gasket replied. "Bones has some contacts in Wagga Wagga. He's taken them up there with Spike until things die down."

"And how long is that going to be?" I demanded, my irritation rising.

"It'll take as long as it takes," Gasket shot back. "Damn, you're impatient, woman. Guns blazing isn't going to help us right now. You saw what happened at the cottage. I don't want a repeat if I can help it."

"Speaking of..." Chaser interrupted. "What happened to the place after we left?"

"It's swarming with cops," the old wolf replied, his voice crackling over the call. "DeLuca went back to scout it out but couldn't get close. The whole area was cordoned off."

"Better to stay away," Chaser agreed.

"What about the bodies?" I asked. "What happened to those? They'd have pack insignia on them and tattoos." I held up my hand and wiggled my thumb at Chaser. "They'll trace them back to us, won't they?"

"I left a couple of guys behind to clean up," Gasket explained. "Not entirely honest, but we can't afford cops on our tail. It'll only complicate things."

I glanced at Chaser, wondering how detailed 'clean up' was. I had a vague recollection of my father's shredded body in the bush.

"Don't worry, Sloane," Chaser said, placing his hand on my thigh. "This isn't a first for us."

"So, what now?" I threw out into the void, hoping I'd like the answer.

"We're going back to the compound to clear it out," Gasket said. "It's only a matter of time before the cops link the cottage to the pack. Then we'll track the rest of the renegades. Chances are they'll make it easy for us and come knocking."

"How do you know they aren't already waiting?" I fretted.

"We've got eyes on the place, Sloane. It's free and clear. Don't worry about us, okay? You've got bigger fish to fillet."

I snorted and rolled my eyes. "You sure you're not a secret agent? You've got some real network there, Gasket."

He laughed, the deep, throaty sound comforting. "Nope. I'm just an old wolf who's been around the block a few times. You haven't been around us long, girl. You'll understand the lupine network soon enough."

It was more confirmation that he was the perfect choice to be alpha of the Fortitude Wolves. To think I had the gall to stand up and throw my hat into the ring. I wasn't leadership material—even as part of a revenge plot.

"I'll be in touch when I have more news," Gasket said. "If you need anything…"

"We'll let you know," Chaser replied.

"Good luck."

Chaser ended the call and put the phone back on the charger.

"So that's it," I murmured. "We're on our own."

"It was always going to be this way."

"Yeah… I still don't like it." I leaned against the wall, propping a pillow behind me. "You and me against all those vampires. I bet King owns a giant skyscraper—a really big one—*and* wears fancy suits and drinks thousand-dollar bottles of wine."

"King has a large stake in the casino in Melbourne," Chaser confirmed. "He owns three-quarters of the *Halcyon*, and he maintains the upper three floors and penthouse as his personal residence."

"That isn't reassuring," I drawled. "It'll be locked up tight."

He snorted and shook his head. "You're right. Security *is* tight. I've never done a job that required me to crack such sophisticated measures."

My ears pricked up at the mention of his work. Chaser hadn't spoken in detail about what he did while he was conscripted into Fortitude, not even before. Mercenary, assassin, *husband*...he'd been all those things.

"Then how do we get close?" I thought about it and began imagining scenarios where we took on different aliases and wore wigs. That might fool security cameras and facial recognition software, but vampires? And what if they had witches? I knew nothing about them or their spells.

"We're going to have to do a lot of surveillance," Chaser said. "You good with that?"

I shrugged. "You know I'm impatient."

It was Chaser's turn to sigh. He stretched out on the bed beside me, throwing an arm around my shoulders. I nestled against him, his presence comforting. I'd almost acclimatised to the dry heat of the plains, though I longed for milder weather.

"Chaser?"

"*Hmm...*" he muttered, tightening his grip around me.

"If we manage to kill King, it won't end there, will it?"

"I don't know..."

"There'll be someone else just waiting to step into his shoes. The Hollow Men won't end with the death of one person."

"Probably not."

"And there'll always be someone coming after me."

He grunted.

I sighed, closing my eyes. The reality of our situation wasn't offering much hope. We could kill King, then the vampire who came after, and then the one who came after that, but it'll still do nothing to change anything. Then there were rival wolf packs who'd do anything to neutralise my power. Someone had better call up the dictionary because futile had a new definition.

It sucked, but I was only now realising that I longed for a life that might never come.

"Chaser?"

"*Hmm*?"

"It's not just King. We have to make sure..."

"I know," he whispered. "We will."

I hoped he was right.

CHAPTER 3
CHASER

I couldn't deny Sloane had changed after the other night. I still didn't know if it was for better or worse, but something had shifted.

That night, I drifted off to sleep beside her. Sometimes the tension was palpable between us. We argued, we called each other names, but it always circled back to calm moments of understanding. Always. Three months wasn't a long time to be with someone and know who they were, but with Sloane and me... Sometimes people just clicked, I guessed.

I fell into the deepest layers of sleep, my subconscious calling to my darkest memories.

The *Halcyon* was a gross example of wealth that always made me want to choke. A doorknob in this hellhole was worth more than I made in an entire year.

"I knew you wouldn't be able to resist playing the

hero," a voice boomed, echoing through the empty theatre.

A spotlight switched on with a heavy click, illuminating the stage. The glittery backdrop sparkled in the sudden shower of light where, not an hour ago, a production of Shakespeare's *A Midsummer Night's Dream* had graced the boards.

Now, it was empty, save for me, King, the unknown number of snipers in the shadows, and my wife. *Loretta.*

King thrust his hand into her chestnut locks and forced her head up. She swallowed a sob...until her gaze met mine. A cry of terror tore from her throat, piercing my heart. Tears streamed down her cheeks, smearing her skin. She was terrified...and it was all my fault.

My grip tightened around the gun in my hand, and with murder on my mind, I stepped forwards. Something metallic pressed into the base of my skull, and I tensed, stopping in my tracks.

"I wouldn't if I were you," a voice said behind me.

"Let this be a lesson to you, *William Mason*," King drawled, pulling a gun from behind his back. "No one crosses me and gets away with it. *No one.*"

He aimed, then fired, the boom tearing through the theatre, and Loretta fell.

"No!" I roared, twisting to the side. I knocked the gun away from me, the vampire startled by my sudden outburst. I fired, the wooden bullet hitting him in the stomach, and sprinted towards the light, but King was already gone.

Vaulting onto the stage, I skidded on my knees and grasped Loretta's shoulders. The bullet had torn through her neck and blood poured from the wound. She gasped for breath, but she was only inhaling blood, the wet, sucking sound choking her to death.

"*No, no, no, no...*" I pressed my palms against the wound, but I knew it was useless. I couldn't stop this; it was beyond my abilities to heal.

Her sightless eyes shone with unshed tears that were trapped in the moment of death.

"Chaser, we've got to go."

I woke with a start, my chest heaving.

Kicking my feet out of bed, I leaned forwards, my elbows digging into my legs. A sob burst unbidden from my throat, the dream clinging to my mind like a parasite.

It had felt so real.

"Chaser?" Sloane's voice was a whisper in the darkness.

Glancing over my shoulder, I saw she was lying among the blankets, her hair splayed across the pillow.

"Chaser..." Her eyes were full of questions I didn't want to answer. "Have you been..." She sat up. "Have you—"

I cut off her question with a grunt and wiped the grit from my eyes.

"Chaser?" she whispered. "What's going on?"

Sloane was here. Sloane was real. *She was real.*

"Nothing," I finally managed. "Go back to sleep."

Her eyes were full of questions. She knew something was different, but like the moron I was, I rolled over and shut her out.

This time when I fell asleep, it was dreamless.

<hr>

It was my turn to sit on the rooftop and pout. Sloane and I had that in common—the sky, the solitary, introspective nonsense.

I'd shut off my humanity completely after Loretta was murdered, choosing to sever contact entirely than to have to feel her loss...and the pain of my forced servitude to the Fortitude Wolves. That was why it was a miracle I felt anything at all for Sloane. I hadn't wanted to turn it back on, but she'd found a way without even trying. *Without even understanding.*

Loretta was human, and I couldn't save her. Sloane was supernatural, but she wasn't immortal.

I leaned back in the lawn chair and kicked my feet up onto the railing. The horizon was filled with brownish smoke from the bushfires that were still burning out of control.

I heard footsteps clanging up the metal staircase behind me. I shot a look over my shoulder and sighed as Sloane's head appeared, her blue aviator sunglasses on her face. Turning back to the view, I said nothing as she approached.

"What are you doing?" she asked, her voice echoing.

"I'm watching the road."

She stepped closer, her boots scuffing on the roof, and I knew another deep and meaningful conversation was incoming. If I wanted to get over all my hang-ups and have a future at all, I knew I had to face a lot of screwed-up things, but avoidance was more attractive right now. I had to be strong until this was all over.

Sloane sat beside me. "What happened last night?"

I said nothing.

"*Chaser.*"

I shrugged.

"You're a hypocrite, you know that?" She sounded angry with me.

I nodded, doing my best to shut my feelings off without totally abandoning them. "Of course, I am."

"Maybe I'm indifferent to the things I've done, but you're not."

"If you're trying to push all my buttons at once, keep going," I said, narrowing my eyes in warning.

She moved closer, her body blocking out the sun, the light haloing around her curves.

"Chaser...you were crying."

"*Shit.* Do you want me to hand you a knife so you can cut off my balls?" I exclaimed.

"If you can't talk to me about these things, then

what are we doing?" she retorted. "You can't keep turning into a wanker every time it gets too hard."

"Yeah, I'm a right cu—"

"Don't say that word," she shot at me. "I hate that word."

"You swear like a sailor, yet you forbid me from saying cu—"

"*Chaser.*"

I rolled my eyes and returned to staring at the comings and goings of the motel below.

"You had a dream about her, didn't you?"

I flinched as Sloane's words hit home.

"You can talk to me, you know. I'm not insecure about it anymore." She dragged a lawn chair across the roof and set it beside mine, then flopped onto the green and white plastic.

"You really want to hear about how I got my wife murdered?" I drawled. "What did I do to deserve you?"

"Don't," she murmured, staring at me over the top of her sunglasses. "Don't do that with me."

I sighed heavily, my eyes still burning with the afterimage of my dream. I wondered what had triggered it. Stress? Too much humanity? *Maybe.*

"When I turned...I was the same age as you are now," I said, staring across the plains. "London, 1891. William Mason, stonemason."

Sloane perked up. "You were a stonemason?"

I nodded. "I worked on the Tower Bridge...until I had a terrible accident on the way home one evening."

A scowl spread across my face as my memory darkened. "As a new vampire, everything was a rush—the speed, strength, even the healing... I thought I was invincible. Why wouldn't I be?" I snorted. "But it was the blood that pushed me over the edge; it was all I ever thought about. I was a junkie with all the enhanced abilities of an apex predator."

I didn't have to explain the rest to her. How King had turned me and left me to become a monster, then drafted me into the Hollow Men—his signature recruitment style—then how I'd met Loretta and fallen in love with her. How we'd conspired to leave it all behind... How King had repaid my betrayal. I'd lost everything in a matter of days. My entire life had turned into one giant mess.

"I was too late to save her, you know that," I went on. "I didn't just hear about her murder. I saw it. I held her in my arms and saw the moment the life left her eyes. I saw the moment..." I shoved away the image that'd stirred me from sleep. "At first, working for the pack was the only thing stopping me from..." I shook my head. "I did messed-up things to forget. Every person I killed had his face. I liked it, Sloane." I glanced at her and was surprised to see tears in her eyes.

"That was before," she murmured. "That's not now."

"King shot her in the neck," I admitted. "The bullet went through and through. She choked on her own blood while I stood in front of her unable to stop it… She was human, and it was too much for me to heal, but I pressed my hands against her neck… King knew she'd bleed out and there'd be nothing I could do about it."

"Chaser…"

"Chaser is a murderer," I snapped. "William was a stupid boy who got his wife killed. What the hell have I done to fix things?"

"We're doing something now," she said firmly. "It's better than nothing at all. I made you a promise, and we'll figure out the rest as we go."

"You made *Chaser* a promise," I scoffed. Who was I supposed to be? William, Chaser, or someone else? Man, husband, good guy, murderer, crook, hostile, *evil incarnate*.

Sloane angled herself towards me, the plastic lawn chair creaking with the movement. "You'll always be Chaser to me. Not because of where you ended up, but because it was the name you first gave me. If you want me to call you William, I can do that."

"William's gone," I whispered.

"I can call you dickhead, how about that?"

My lips quirked.

"See? There's something in there after all." She slapped my arm and leaned back in her chair. "What a pair we are."

She was uncanny with the way she turned things around.

"The Hollow Men have a stake in the casino, you say?" she mused.

"The *Halcyon*."

"You were a part of them," she went on. "That's valuable. The pain will last a little while longer, but instead of using it to forget, use it to *remember*."

"I know," I said. "I've shut it out for so long... The first rush stings, you know."

Sloane shuffled next to me and kicked her feet up onto the railing next to mine. I studied our boots and relaxed slightly when she let her knees fall to the side and press against my legs.

"Have you..." I began, my uncertainty throwing my resolve sideways.

"I never shut any of it out," she murmured, staring out over the desert. "I percolate in misery and pain like a Sylvia Plath novel. Maybe that's why I'm so *whatever* about the last few months. It hurts, but I can take it."

I snorted and couldn't imagine her reading a book of miserable poetry. She did have that huge textbook, so maybe it wasn't so farfetched...

"We'll be all right, Chaser," she said. "You'll be all right. One last job, just remember that."

I grunted and leaned my arm on the side of her chair, facing my palm towards the sky. She slipped her hand into mine, and I caressed the tattoo on her thumb. The crossed swords meant something else now, even though the motto was the same.

Courage in adversity.

CHAPTER 4

SLOANE

Chaser's admission caused all kinds of messed-up thoughts to swirl in my mind.

I knew he wasn't able to save Loretta, but if she'd been able to fight, would her fate have changed? I didn't know enough about her to answer that question. I knew I had the strength to pull the trigger if I had to, but in a situation like that, where I only had my fists against a vampire...? I wasn't so sure.

People could stew over what-ifs their whole lives and never be prepared for the future. In the grand scheme of things, I didn't know much at all. I was just a woman who'd become brilliant at hiding. Scratch that. Chaser had found me, so maybe it was just another thing I was fooling myself with.

"Chaser?"

"Hmm?"

"I want you to teach me how to fight."

Chaser glanced at me, the lawn chair he was sitting on creaking. I hoped it didn't break under his weight. All the furniture up here was so sun-bleached, even the metal had turned brittle.

"I can fire a gun, but all the other stuff..." I shrugged. "It's just... We're going to be here for a little while yet, and I know I've kicked a few bad guys in the balls already, but I can't help thinking it was all just dumb luck."

Chaser threw a look over his shoulder, his skin glistening with sweat. "Up here?"

"Where else?"

"You'd have to get a tetanus shot if you got cut."

"Don't wrap me in cotton wool, Chaser." I rolled my eyes and let my head fall back. "I'm a werewolf. I'd be surprised if I needed a tetanus shot at all."

"You're the last person who needs cotton wool," he drawled, grasping my thigh.

I wondered about Loretta. I remembered the woman from the photograph Chaser had in his wallet and couldn't picture the man he was now with a sweet-looking woman like her.

"What was she like?"

He tensed, but didn't pull away. "You really want to know?"

I couldn't imagine what he'd felt when he saw Loretta die. I knew he was worried about the effect shooting Marini had on me, but it was different. The man was my father, but I never loved him—not since I was that innocent little girl whose mother tried to shield her from the brutal reality of her life. Besides, I'd come to terms with his betrayal a long time ago. What Chaser went through was different; he genuinely loved his wife.

I didn't know if I was being stupid or not, but I was still jealous of a woman who'd died a hundred years ago. At least a little bit. She still haunted his dreams.

"I suppose I don't."

"It's not a competition, Sloane."

"Wherever there's a roof, you seem to find it," I said, ignoring his statement. "Why's that?"

"I like high places," he replied with a shrug.

"You can see the stars better up here at night."

Chaser glanced up to where the moon hung, a white wisp against the blue sky. "It's a perspective thing."

"Perspective would be helping me prepare before heading into one of the many layers of Hell," I quipped. "As much as I love our fighting and these deep, meaningful conversations you loathe so much, I need to be able to protect myself. I still don't know the breadth of my abilities when I'm not a wolf, and I need to understand that part of me. What if we're separated like we were on the train?"

"It's my job to protect you."

"Nuh-uh, it *was* your job. Now it's our spiritual right to protect one another."

Chaser snorted, his lips quirking.

"Besides, it'll give us something to keep our minds off the avalanche of shit hurtling towards us."

"Well, when you say it like that..."

He rose from the lawn chair and held out his hand. I grasped it, and he pulled me upright before kicking away the chairs.

"We'll be okay up here?" I asked, shielding my eyes from the sun.

"No one can see much of anything," Chaser replied, clearing away some of the ruined furniture. "I haven't seen a single person come up here." He pointed towards the main office. "I overheard the bloke at the desk saying the place is only at a quarter capacity. We're good."

"You're good at 'overhearing.'" It helped he had supernatural abilities.

"*Surveillance*," he corrected. "We don't want to draw too much unwanted attention."

"Brilliant," I drawled. "I don't want anyone seeing me get my arse kicked, so that's perfect."

"With vampires, you only have a second to react," he began. "A fight is about gaining control and dominating, even if it's just about getting away and not—"

"Killing?"

"Yeah, that." He pursed his lips before he continued, "Aim for the parts of the body where you can do the most damage while anticipating his or her moves."

"Sounds easy when you put it like that," I said.

"It takes a lot of practice. Whatever you do, don't step any closer than you have to. Here," he said, wrapping his fingers around my wrist. "When you go for the upper half of the body, use your hand. Your palm goes up to crack the nose, and the outer edge can strike the neck. Or a fist to the throat." He pressed his fist under the curve of my ribcage, putting light pressure beneath my lungs. "With enough force, you can push the air out of your attacker's lungs...even a vampire's."

His pointers made sense. I thought about some of the situations I'd found myself in, and an image came back to me of the night I'd first met Chaser. I'd intended to pack up and leave rather than be dragged back to Fortitude, but unfortunately, the Hollow Men had found me first.

"Do you remember that night at the *Sailor's Arms*?" I asked. "When..." I gestured, my hands waving in the air. "You know..."

"*I know.*"

"How would I get out of that?"

"Bent over with a knife at your throat?" He raised his eyebrows. "With a lot of trouble."

I glanced away. "So, I was screwed..."

"Sometimes, you've got to take a hit to get out of a situation."

"You think I should've let him..." I choked and felt like giving him a black eye.

"I'm talking about the knife." He strode towards me and curled his hand around the back of my neck, then tugged me forwards. "Know where your veins are. This one..." he traced a line down what I supposed was my jugular, "you protect. You'll bleed out in seconds if it gets cut. If you tilt your head the other way slightly, you just get a knick, but you gain ground on your attacker."

I nodded, swallowing hard. "Maybe we should...try something else."

Chaser's eyes darkened, and I felt his free hand trail a line down my back.

"How do you kill a vampire?"

"A stake in the heart," Chaser replied, letting me go. "Though anything wood will do. Bullets are most effective, as you already know."

"That's the only way?"

He nodded. "Everything else is temporary. A snapped neck heals. A vampire who's bled out can be revived with blood. Drowning..."

My gaze moved to the horizon, where smoke still smudged the blue. "What about fire?"

Chaser shrugged. "That *can* kill us...if it's to the point of incineration."

"A technicality."

"You can't heal ashes."

I pushed away an unexpected image of Chaser burning. "What's the fastest way to the heart?"

"With a stake, underneath the ribcage and upwards." He pressed his palm against my stomach.

"Here...and here." He pressed his fingers into my back, showing me. "Going through the chest is ill-advised. Too much bone in the way."

I rubbed the heel of my palm between my breasts. "The sternum."

"It's a hard plate of bone, impossible to penetrate... unless you get lucky and hit between the ribs."

"A gun with wooden bullets is better?"

"It is, but you can't count on having one."

That's why he was advising on escape manoeuvres. The best way to fight a vampire was not to fight one at all, but for us it was going to be an inevitability.

"My werewolf abilities," I said. "You've been around wolves for a century, so you know what I'm supposed to be able to do."

"You already do most of it," he told me. "You just don't believe in yourself."

"I believe enough."

Chaser snorted.

"But—"

"Sloane, you're not bound by the moon. You're strong always."

I sighed in frustration. "I know, but what does that mean?"

He nodded towards the edge of the roof. "Jump and find out."

"What?" I blinked, not understanding what he meant.

"*Jump.*"

I looked over the edge of the roof and grimaced. He wanted me to jump down there?

"What?" the vampire asked, rolling his eyes. "You afraid or something?"

I jutted out my chin. "I'm not afraid. What if somebody sees?"

"No one's around."

"What if I fall?" I asked.

He smirked and sauntered to the edge. "You'll heal."

"*Chaser.*"

"I'll go first. If you fall, I'll catch you."

I eyeballed him. "Promise?"

"It would be anti-climactic if I let you die now."

Before I could answer, he leapt off the roof and landed at the bottom, making it look easy. He turned and spread his arms wide, waiting.

I couldn't believe I was entertaining this. Jumping off a roof seemed so... I couldn't even say the word. Chaser seemed to think I could make it without breaking both ankles, but I wasn't so sure.

Courage, Sloane. You can do this. You turn into a wolf, for crying out loud.

Taking a deep breath, I jumped.

Air rushed past my face and I landed, my knees bending slightly as my boots connected with the asphalt. I'd expected a painful jarring to splinter through my legs, but I barely felt a whisper.

Straightening, I looked at Chaser. He was leaning against the wall, smirking.

"You didn't even try to catch me!" I exclaimed.

"Because I knew you'd make it."

"*Arsehole!*"

His smirk turned into a grin. "Did you have fun?"

My anger began to subside and my gaze moved to the roof above. *Yeah, it* had *been fun.*

"You have the strength to do that and more..." he went on, "if you have faith in yourself."

"Like what?"

"You can run faster and farther than you ever thought possible. You can jump higher than a man, heal almost any wound, see, hear, smell—"

"But I'm not faster or stronger than a vampire."

Chaser's smirk faded as he shook his head. "But you're not easy prey, either."

"That's why I want to learn to fight." I stepped into the shade before my skin burnt. "To know where to strike."

"Hopefully you won't have to strike at all."

I opened my mouth to argue, but he shook his head. "C'mon," Chaser said. "Let's go inside."

The motel room was dark and slightly cooler than the furnace of the outside world. Taking off my sunglasses, I tossed them onto the table where they slid across the surface before coming to rest beside the revolver. I tensed, a strange melancholy coming over me.

"You okay?" Chaser asked, closing the door and blocking out the last of the burning sunlight.

"Yeah...just tired, I guess." Picking up the revolver, I stroked my thumb over the mother-of-pearl. "Taking a life... It's so final."

Chaser nodded, prying the gun from my grasp. "What we need to do to survive isn't easy."

What was that thing Sam told me about Harley? He'd been a good man once. Well, as good as he was able to be under the circumstances. Fortitude changed him for the worse, tapping into his violent tendencies and amplifying them. What if the same thing was happening to me? This whole plan to take out my father, then King... What if I was headed down the same path? One kill had become two, and there would be more. How many people did I have to murder before I lost myself? *Before I became Marini...*

"I don't want... I don't want to turn into Harley." I glanced at Chaser, who narrowed his eyes.

"You don't want to turn into me?"

"No, I didn't mean... It was something Sam had told me before she left. This life turned him into a monster..."

"She told me the same thing," Chaser said. "Don't worry, Sloane. I know what happened to me, and that's why I push you to confront things. That's why I'd prefer to take the gun out of your hands and take your place. I don't want you to go through the things I have...especially not because of me."

"I know. I..." I glanced at the revolver. "It's not who I killed. It's the fact that I killed in the first place."

Chaser cupped my face and rubbed his thumb across my cheek. "I don't want to say it'll get easier because it won't. Just..."

"Just what?"

"Just don't do what I did. Don't shut it out."

I nodded slightly, leaning into his palm.

"Promise me."

"I can't," I whispered.

Chaser's intentions were noble, but I knew I was going to have to go to an even darker place before this was over. I just hoped to hell I wouldn't lose my soul along the way.

CHAPTER 5

CHASER

I squinted at the mobile phone screen, angling the map in different directions.

The *Halcyon Casino and Resort* was the ultimate in luxury—a five-star hotel sitting above a bustling casino, home to theatres, restaurants, shopping, and high-class gambling.

On the surface, it looked just like any other casino, which it was to the foot traffic that wandered in off the street, but I knew the vampiric vibe resonated the deeper into the building people went. I wondered if any of them came out again with their bodies and minds intact...if they came out at all.

Sloane rolled over on the bed behind me and sighed. I felt the same way. All the talking over the past couple of days had left me emotionally exhausted. My humanity was more than intact, the frayed edges healed enough that the rush of feeling didn't quite overwhelm me anymore—not unless I was unprepared for it.

"What are you doing?" she asked, sitting beside me.

"We need to get to work," I replied. "We can't wait for Gasket. It's not realistic."

"Now who's getting impatient."

"The pack could be dealing with the renegades for years," I went on. "They could have joined a rival pack or be devising a strike on the compound. We can't bank on their help with the Hollow Men. Besides, there are still things we can do while waiting for the heat to die down."

"I know," Sloane said in agreement. "What do you have in mind?"

"It's been a long time since I was a part of the vampire world. Things would have changed. The best place to start is contacting some old *friends* from my Hollow Men days."

Her brow creased. "Is that smart?"

"It's a risk, but the Hollow Men know our faces. We can't just walk into that casino and expect not to be picked up on the security feeds. They'll have facial recognition, not to mention help from witches."

"What kind of help?"

"Spells to detect intruders, wards to keep people in...and a thousand other things."

She sighed, realising our predicament. "So, we need another way in."

"I know a guy. It's a long shot, but he might have some actionable information."

"A vampire?"

"Yeah. I kept in touch with him for a while after Loretta died," I explained. "I'd planned to go back in and finish King off, but other things got in the way. It's been a long time, but I think it's worth the risk. He wanted to see the Hollow Men dismantled as much as we do."

"Common enemy..." she mused. "Can you be certain he still feels the same way after a century?"

I shrugged. "Time moves differently for vampires."

"I can't even fathom a hundred years," she said uncertainly. "I don't like it."

"Like I said, it's a long shot. The guy was flaky back then, and when he realised I wasn't going to do anything about King, he split."

"So now that we're on the hunt, he might want back in?"

"Assuming he's still around."

"Okay, so when are we going?"

I glanced at her and narrowed my eyes. There was no way in hell I was putting Sloane in a vulnerable position. She didn't need to be there, getting her face more known than it already was.

"No," I said. "You'll stay here."

"What did I say about wrapping me in cotton wool?" she exclaimed. "I want to go. I need to be a part of this, Chaser."

"And I don't need you to wave yourself underneath the noses of our enemy," I replied, keeping a lid on my anger. "The same enemy who wants to sacrifice you for ultimate power." I admired her strength, but there was this thing she had with letting it snowball into stubbornness. "Besides, I don't trust him. There's a chance he'll pull a double cross the moment I show my face. Allegiances can be bought."

She hissed and leaned back in the chair, resting her foot in front of her. Hugging her knee, she eyed me warily. "I don't like it."

"It's a risk…"

"A really big one. When are you going?"

"Now," I replied.

"*Now?*"

"If I want to catch him unawares, I need to make this a fast turnaround. The less chance he's got to rat me out, the better."

Sloane sighed and her shoulders slumped.

"We'll only get one chance at this," I murmured. "We've gotta do it right."

"I know. I'm just…worried about you."

I rested my forehead against hers and traced the curve of her lips with my thumb, studying the dusting of freckles across her nose and cheeks, and breathed in her scent.

"If you get into trouble, activate the talisman," I told her. "I'll pull the plug and come back."

She took my face in her hands. "It's not me I'm worried about..."

"This is what I do," I murmured. "I'll be fine."

<hr>

It was a five-hour drive from Mallee to Melbourne.

I was already missing the isolation of rural Victoria by the time I reached the city limits. The noise, the people, the *smells*... All of them I could do without. It was easier to deal with it all without humanity, but if I let it go again, everything I felt for Sloane would disappear.

She's safe, I thought. *She'll be fine until I get back.*

Monroe's was a classic American diner that sat on the corner of a busy intersection in the south of the city, but it may as well have been in another world. Watching the building from across the street, I wasn't surprised to find the place empty. Back in the day, it used to be bustling. There would be a row of motorcycles sitting out front, a brawl would spill out onto the footpath at least once a week—a brawl that was compelled out of the mind of law enforcement— and the bacon, eggs, and blood-laced cherry pie flowed like the information Monroe himself gathered for the highest bidder. Until the Hollow Men tightened the screws. That had a lot to do with me—back when I was a soldier under King's thumb, unfortunately—but I wasn't a remorseful kind of guy.

Thirty minutes waiting in the sun was enough for me. I crossed the street and slinked down a laneway a few buildings down, then circled back towards the diner. Waiting by the bin wasn't my idea of a good time, but Monroe would have to come out eventually.

Fortunately, I didn't have to wait long. The back door opened, and the vampire stepped out, carrying a full garbage bag.

He was a tall, lean, African American, who'd come to Australia by way of the southern states in the early twentieth century. I didn't know much about his past, save for he'd been taken from his homeland and sold as a slave in the Caribbean, then trafficked to the American mainland soon after. How he'd become a vampire was a mystery. All I knew, was the man he was now—a peddler of supernatural information, or at least he was when I'd last seen him.

I watched as he lifted the trash into the dumpster, bottles clinking. Didn't he know recycling was a thing these days?

I coughed, and the vampire jumped, spinning on his heel.

"William Mason," he drawled the moment his gaze met mine. "Aren't you a sight for sore eyes."

"Still shovelling vampire shit, I see," I retorted, leaning against the wall. "You're getting sloppy."

"I thought you'd be six feet under by now." He shook his head and closed the lid on the dumpster. Reaching into his breast pocket, he pulled out a pack of cigarettes and flipped it open. He offered one to me, and I shook my head. "Shit, and you gone straight, too. No smoke?"

"I quit."

"You quit a lot of things, I see. Last I heard, you were running with a pack of flea-bitten mongrels."

"Life has a messed-up way of coming full circle."

Monroe eyed me, then glanced up and down the lane. "Come in. It's hot out here."

Vampires didn't feel the heat, and he confirmed what I already knew. The diner was being watched.

He opened the back door for me, and I stepped into the dreary diner. The kitchen was just as empty as the front, and the sole waitress could be seen through the partition, mopping the floor of the restaurant. *Definitely seen better days.*

"Heather, take a break!" Monroe called out.

The waitress scowled and dumped the mop, letting it clatter to the floor. She muttered something foul under her breath and stormed out of the diner. A second later, the bell rang furiously, then the door slammed.

"Raging bitch, that one," Monroe drawled. "Good thing I can compel her. You want a drink?"

I nodded, and he turned to take a soft drink bottle from the refrigerator. Opening the lid, he placed the Coke in front of me.

I raised my eyebrows.

"What?" Monroe drawled. "I lost my liquor license."

"It's a little vanilla for my tastes," I told him, knowing he could just compel himself a new license... unless King was blocking him.

"Just take the damn Coke, Chaser," he said, settling on the chair opposite. "So, what is it this time? I'm getting too damned old for this shit."

"You're barely three hundred," I replied, curling my hand around the cool bottle.

"You know me, Will. Without this pile-of-shit diner, I'd be out on the street."

"So, nothing's changed?"

He inclined his head. "Once you're in, you never leave."

I snorted and took a sip of Coke. Bubbles ran down my throat, doing nothing to quench the burn I felt. Alcohol would be good right now...blood, better.

"Why are you here?" Monroe asked. "You never stop by for a friendly chat."

He was right. Things never got personal between us, though when I was still with the Hollow Men, I did my best to keep the heat off the guy. Back then, *Monroe's* had been the go-to place for the supernatural dregs of society. A bad-news kind of place.

It wasn't spoken aloud, but Monroe had always been under the Hollow Men's thumb. They ran this part of the city, while the Fortitude Wolves controlled the north.

"They tried to hurt someone close to me," I said. There was no use hiding my reasons. They weren't unique in the slightest. Revenge was a mill that kept on grinding around here.

Monroe raised his eyebrows and blew through his teeth. "Again? Once wasn't enough for you?"

"Believe me, it's a situation I'd rather not be in."

"So, I assume you want to go back in?"

"Like you said, I never stop by for a friendly chat."

"Who's buying?"

"I pay in blood, you know that."

"Only because you don't have King's backing anymore."

"What good is influence when your enemies are still breathing?"

"No deal." Monroe stood and pointed towards the door. "You know how things work around here. Get your sorry arse out of my diner, or I'll have to let them know you were here."

I smiled up at him, realising he *was* old. Not in the age sense, three hundred wasn't ancient for a vampire, but living his life on the edge of the law—vampiric *and* human—had worn him down. His skin was sallow, his eyes watery, and there were lines around his brow and mouth usually reserved for old men. He was underfed and full of fear.

"How long have you had this place?" I asked, staring up at him. "Established...1910?"

"William, I'm warning you."

"I noticed a distinct lack of customers on the way in. The economic downturn doesn't cater for bacon, eggs, and refillable coffee, does it?"

"What are you getting at, boy?"

"It's a metaphor, Monroe," I drawled, smiling at the fact that he'd called me *boy*. "You're becoming obsolete. Instead of rolling in dirty money, you're barely keeping the doors open. The world has moved on, the humans have gotten smarter, and compulsion no longer cuts it."

"Are you threatening me?"

"Depends on how you look at it. I like to view it as an *offer*."

His eyes narrowed. "Which is?"

"You get me a way into the Hollow Men's operation, I'll get you out of Melbourne and set you up. I know a crew who'd appreciate bacon and eggs."

Monroe snorted and sat back down. I had him.

"What kind of crew?"

"Fortitude."

"A werewolf pack? *No way in hell*." He waved me off. "You want to put me under the thumb of another madman?"

I grinned, thinking about Sloane and Gasket. "It's under new management."

"Marini...?"

"Is dead."

Monroe scratched his head and frowned, the cogs in his mind working overtime.

"Changes things, right?" I raised my eyebrows, waiting for his answer.

As I saw it, he didn't have much choice. Even in Fortitude's current state of turmoil, it was a far sight better than waiting for the diner to go completely under. That was, if the Hollow Men didn't decide putting a bullet in his heart was better for everyone. With the pack, Monroe had a chance for a better life. One that could be a family to him, despite being what he was. Wolves were like that, much more than vampires.

"I know you, Monroe," I continued. "You're not a bad guy. You're just a victim of circumstance, profiting the only way you know how. When I knew you before, you wanted to get out. You wanted out so badly, you were willing to sell out King. Well, here's your last chance."

"How do I know you won't cross me again?"

"You don't."

I stared at him as he stewed over my proposition. Asking a man like Monroe to have faith was like asking for the impossible, but put him between a rock and a hard place...

"I can tell you what I know, but it isn't much," he warned. "Like you said, times have changed."

I downed the last of my Coke and slammed the glass bottle onto the table.

"I'll take whatever I can get."

CHAPTER 6
SLOANE

Chaser had been gone a long time.

I leaned back in the green and white plastic lawn chair, watching as the last of the sun lowered past the horizon. Only a thin sliver of burning orange lingered, and the longer I stared at it, the more its image burned into my retinas. I closed my eyes and chased the afterimage around the insides of my lids before opening them again.

Sighing, I counted the brightest stars in the sky. *One, two, three, four...* I wished I had a book or that there was something decent on TV, or that the TV actually worked and wasn't all static and noise. I didn't know anything about setting up a reconnaissance mission, so I couldn't even help Chaser plan. There'd been no more word from Gasket, either.

There wasn't much in the way of life out here. After spending the last week watching the comings and goings of the motel, I'd figured out it was more of a rest stop catering to truckers and wayward souls than anything else.

A few hundred metres down the road was the town centre, which consisted of a row of ramshackle shops —a bakery, a tiny IGA supermarket, a newsagent, and a two-pump petrol station.

Chaser had become a regular customer at the IGA, but I'd never been down there. I hadn't left the motel grounds since we'd arrived. It wasn't because I didn't want to—I'd established my impatience factor over and over—it was because Chaser didn't trust that everything and everyone in the outside world wasn't in league with the Hollow Men.

Like anyone out here was working for The Man. Pfft.

My stomach growled, and I looked up at the sky. The stars were well and truly out, even though the thin strip of sunlight still lingered on the horizon. Chaser was taking his sweet time.

I peeled my arse cheeks off the lawn chair and made my way downstairs. Noting the car wasn't parked out front, I scowled and went inside our room. We had to have some food kicking around.

I opened the mouldy refrigerator and squinted at the lone can of beer. Liquid dinner? I made a face and closed the door. If my choices were beer or beer, I'd choose nothing at all. Ironically, those were the only options in the whole stinking place.

Glancing around the room, I thought about going

to the IGA. I wasn't a prisoner here, and the likelihood of someone recognising me out here was slim to none. The nearest town with a population in triple digits was at least forty minutes away, and there was a lot of flat nothingness and farmland between us.

I knew Chaser would be angry about me wandering the town on my own, but as my stomach squelched and popped, I figured he could go screw himself. I could look after myself now that I was a full werewolf.

I snatched up my little coin purse and counted out the money Chaser had left me. Fifty dollars. That ought to get me a mountain of snacks to fatten myself up with. Hesitating, I wondered if I should leave a note. If he came back, and I wasn't here... Well, things would be bad.

I took out the pen from the bedside table and tore a corner off an old newspaper. Over the black and white ink, I scrawled a 'be right back' message and left it on the table.

Outside, the motel grounds were deader than a doornail. Curling my hands into the sleeves of my cardigan, I darted across the road and walked towards the IGA. Nights got cold out here, which never quite made sense to me. A car zoomed past, blowing my hair away from my face, and I glanced over my shoulder at the receding tail lights.

Being out here kind of felt daring. Remembering how it was out on the road with Chaser the first time, I shivered. That was a different story to the one we were in now, but I still erred on the side of caution.

A set of iron horse sculptures that had rusted to a lovely shade of coppery-brown loomed outside the supermarket. I gave them a cursory glance as I passed, my boots scuffing the scrappy little tufts of grass that were trying to grow in the arid soil. Maybe when this was all over, I'd learn to ride a horse, but not here. Someplace cooler where people owned coats. Tasmania, maybe? There were horses in Tasmania, they got snow and ice, and it was far away from here.

I was a dozen steps away from the door when I felt something change in the air. A static charge crackled across my skin, popping and fizzing.

Turning, I saw a woman step out of the shadows, her long blonde hair fluttering in the breeze. Her eyes were filled with fire, and something inside me ignited in response.

Witch.

The wolf within me began to snap as another shadow hurtled out of the darkness and collided with the woman. They powered through the light and slammed into the brick wall of the IGA, sending a dull bang across the silent street.

Chaser held the witch against the wall, his hand curled tightly around her slim neck. She gasped and clawed at his hand, but she had no hope of dislodging the grip of a vampire as strong as him.

"Chaser!" I exclaimed, my eyes widening.

"I told you to stay at the motel," he growled, his blackened eyes never leaving the witch. He bared his fangs at the woman. "Explain yourself before I rip your head off."

She said nothing. I had a chance to study her, to weigh her intentions, but I couldn't figure it out. She was pretty with her long blonde hair and stormy-blue eyes, giving off a bohemian, surf-chic style with her flowing tank top, crystal jewellery, and silver rings...but there was a terrible anger in her my wolf could scent like a bad smell.

"I'd talk if I were you," Chaser snarled. "And *fast*."

She jerked against his hand and scowled. "I had Marini's blood and instead of him, it led me to *her*."

My heart skipped a beat. It was the witch my father had been working with before his demise. The witch who was going to bind the Hollow Men's bloodline. Had she come to finish the job?

"The wolf you were helping him turn into a weapon," Chaser snapped. "His own *daughter*."

"Against my will, just so you know," I said. "I can think of a thousand other things I'd rather be doing besides being slaughtered in a blood ritual."

"Why?" Chaser demanded. "Why were you working with him?"

She curled her lip, choosing to remain silent.

"Revenge," I murmured. "It's always revenge."

The witch let her hands fall to her sides, giving in

to Chaser's hold. "If they took everything from you, you'd do the same."

"*They did*," Chaser said, tightening his grip. "And even if killing Sloane was the only way to pay them back, *I wouldn't*. Do you really think you're the only one the Hollow Men screwed over? Do you really think you're that special?"

"Just do it," the witch hissed. "Kill me. I've got nothing left."

People did desperate, reckless, stupid things when they were hurting. I knew all about that. Trying to run from Chaser on the train, then getting captured and him killed was a prime example. Whoever this witch was, she was in pain. Who had she lost? Her coven? Her family? A lover? It could be anyone, but someone she loved enough to go to war and numb herself to the collateral damage.

There could be hope in all that despair...I'd certainly found some, despite being the target of a supernatural power struggle.

"Let her go," I said. "She doesn't deserve it."

Chaser looked at me, his eyes blackened.

I laid my hand on his shoulder and looked at the witch. "You're wrong. While you live, there's always a chance for something else, something better. You just have to have the strength to try."

Tears filled her eyes. "I have no strength..."

I moved my hand to Chaser's wrist and urged him

to let her go. As his fingers loosened, colour returned to her cheeks.

"Then take some of mine," I told her. "There's another way, and we're going to find it. We can help one another."

"You'd let me go?" she whispered. "I was going to take you to them."

"I know," I told her. "Yet here we are."

A tear trickled down her cheek.

I smiled. "What's your name?"

"Wren..." Her gaze moved to Chaser.

"Forget about him. He's got a leash." I narrowed my eyes at him before nodding towards the IGA. "You hungry? I'm going to get some snacks."

Chaser stared at us and scratched his head. "What the hell just happened?" I heard him mutter, but I wasn't listening.

"Chocolate," I said to Wren. "I reckon we should get some chocolate."

Chaser stood at the door of the motel room, glaring at the witch who was sitting at the table.

I shot him a warning glare and turned to Wren, who was crinkling the wrapper of the Cherry Ripe chocolate bar I'd bought her.

I studied her for a long moment, trying to figure her out.

"So..." I began. "Witches, huh? What's up with that?"

She blinked and glanced at Chaser.

"She's new to all this," he told her.

I snorted. "I only found out there was a supernatural world like two months ago, and now I'm the centre of a war for my blood...or something like that. Honestly, the details are a little hazy." I leaned back in my chair. "Basically, I found out I won the werewolf lottery only to be slapped with a ninety-percent arsehole tax. You know, all that vampire immortality ritual stuff. So, that's me. What about you?"

"I, uh..." Wren set the chocolate bar on the table. "My coven was indentured to the Hollow Men before I was born." She hesitated, her eyes shifting to Chaser. "But we wanted out, knowing there was a chance we'd be killed for trying."

I frowned, knowing where it was going before she even told us. Wren's story was only foreshadowing what would happen to us if we failed.

"They killed them all," she went on. "My parents, my sister and her husband...their son. The only reason I was spared was because I wasn't home." She shrugged. "I've been in hiding ever since."

"That's why you teamed up with my father," I murmured. "Revenge."

"If I'd known you were his daughter..." Her gaze flickered between me and Chaser.

"You still would've done it," Chaser drawled.

"I get it," I said to her, ignoring the surly vampire by the door. "They took your entire family. They took my mother too, and now we're at war with them."

Her eyes narrowed. "What are you going to do with me?"

My eyebrows rose. "Do with you?"

"She thinks we're going to kill her," Chaser drawled. "Which might be worth considering..."

"Chaser!" I exclaimed. "We're not killing anybody!"

He said nothing and turned back to the door, watching the darkness.

"Wren," I said, leaning towards her, "we want the same thing here. If there's another way to take down King and the Hollow Men without turning me into a magical blood bomb, then we're going to figure it out. The only choice you have to make is if you want in or not. We could do with your help. I know vampires and wolves, but witches...? You're the first one I've ever met."

"And if I want out?" Her shoulders tensed and I was sure her expression was softening.

"Then you walk out of here...but you have to leave the Cherry Ripe."

"And if we ever see you again, I'll kill you myself," Chaser snapped.

The room filled with thick silence, and I waited as Wren mulled it over. I wondered how witches got their magic. I had questions about my werewolf heritage, but hers was rather exciting.

Finally, she stirred. "I have nowhere else to go."

"So, that's a yes, then?" I asked.

Wren nodded. "I'll help you...for my family."

I nodded, knowing we hadn't won her trust entirely. Not just yet, anyway. It'd take way more than a heart-to-heart and a Cherry Ripe, but I was determined to try. I wasn't going to do this the Marini way, with blood, violence, and no thought for collateral damage. This war would be won by treading a different path or not at all.

The first step was to show her a weakness she could either use against us...or help us with.

"What can you tell us about this?" I asked, setting the talisman on the table. "Can the spell on it be broken?"

Chaser flew across the room, moving from the door to table in the blink of an eye. "*Sloane.*"

I held up my hand. "Shut up, Chaser."

Wren picked up the bone and turned it over, rubbing her thumb over the markings. "These sigils... They're old."

"*Yeah*, a hundred years," Chaser drawled.

"It's a binding spell entangled with some kind of compulsion... There's an anchor someplace. I can sense threads reaching towards something, but I can't see what." She shook her head and pursed her lips. "This magic was cast by an entire coven. One witch can't undo that kind of magic." She set the bone down and looked at me. "I can't help you."

My heart sank. And entire coven? Where would we find one of those? Nowhere.

"If the spell can't be removed, then can it be destroyed?" I asked.

"No. And I wouldn't try, either."

"Why?"

"Whatever or *whoever* that thing is binding will feel everything you do to it." Her gaze moved to Chaser.

He snorted. "That's a real help."

Wren glared at him, her fear turning into confidence as her true self began to shine through. "Then I suggest you hide it where no one will ever find it."

I picked up the talisman and turned it over in my palm. Where could we stash it? I wasn't about to keep carrying it around with us on our mission to take out King. The last thing we needed was for it to end up in the wrong hands. A safety deposit box seemed a little cliché...

"We put it back where it came from," Chaser said with a grunt.

My gaze lifted. "Put it back?"

"No one will be able to take it from us then," he said, glancing at Wren. "Can it be done?"

The witch nodded. "It'll hurt."

"I can handle it."

"Tomorrow," I said, slipping the talisman into the

safety of my shirt sleeve. "I think we can all do with some rest tonight." I handed Wren back the Cherry Ripe.

"Can't wait," Chaser drawled.

I smiled at the witch as warmly as I could manage. "Thank you, Wren."

"O-okay?" She looked bewildered, her eyes shifting between us.

"You're welcome." I laughed, feeling more hopeful about our situation than I had in days.

All Chaser did was frown...and rub his forearm.

<hr>

I stood on the roof, watching the highway. Darkness wrapped the little town like a thick blanket, the sparse spattering of light barely breaking the absoluteness.

I'd made Chaser get Wren her own room for the night so we could have some alone time. I knew he wanted to tear me a new one over bringing her into the fold, but I was done leaning on others. I had to take charge of my destiny. Wren could help us, and right now, the only thing we could do was take care of our biggest weakness—the talisman.

"I can't believe you just let her in and told her all our secrets," Chaser said behind me. "The talisman—"

"You don't get to turn into a controlling boyfriend," I interrupted, trying to keep my voice from rising. "This is a partnership, Chaser. It's my life, too."

"We're not playing a game," he fired back.

"I know what's at stake! We've been talking about it for weeks!"

"Then what aren't you understanding? Why did you leave when I told you to stay put?"

"I was hungry, Chaser. I didn't know when you were coming back, so I went to get something to eat. *Deal with it.*" I wasn't going to apologise for leaving the room or make excuses for my lack of understanding of witches. "You were gone for over twenty hours."

"I had to work a deal," he said. "And it's a ten-hour round trip. That's why it took so long."

"What deal?"

He sighed and leaned against the railing. "Fortitude has a new live-in cook."

I made a face. "*Okay?*"

"The guy... The informant was almost no good. His importance to the Hollow Men was almost non-existent, but he was able to give me a few leads."

"So, in exchange for getting him out of the city and setting him up with a cushy job with burly bodyguards, you got us a couple of maybes?" I curled my lip. "Seems like a bad deal to me."

"It's better than nothing."

"We'll see about that," I muttered.

Chaser snorted. "I have a vampire cook and you have a broken-hearted witch. Are we even now?"

"*Not even half.*"

He tensed but didn't bite back.

"Wren will help us with the talisman, then we can help her…by helping ourselves. We all want the same thing, Chaser." I laid a hand on his shoulder. "We have to take care of one another. It doesn't matter if we're all different species. We're not going to segregate our problems anymore. The Hollow Men have terrorised *everyone*. It's not just about me and my curse-free blood anymore. They have to be stopped."

Chaser looked up at me, the anger in his eyes fading. "And you say you're not ready to be alpha."

I sighed. "I'm not. One clever statement doesn't make me a leader."

"It's a start."

"Just like trusting Wren."

He snorted. "And all I have to do is let the witch who conspired to have you murdered cut open my arm, break my bones, and implant a magical talisman inside me."

"*It's a start*," I said firmly, wrapping my arm around his waist.

"Who knows? It might be better than a wooden bullet to the heart."

We stood together for a while, watching the stars. It certainly felt like the calm before the storm.

"So, what now?" I asked. "What are we going to do with your maybe leads?"

"After we deal with the talisman," Chaser said, "we go back to the city and see if Monroe is full of shit or not."

"Already?"

He nodded. "It's time to head into the city."

"For real?" My stomach churned in a different kind of way.

"For real."

CHAPTER 7

SLOANE

The sun rose the next morning in a blaze of burnt red and orange. The smear of bushfire smoke was dissipating, but I could still smell it in the air—charred wood and eucalyptus.

Leaning against the railing on the edge of the motel roof, I sighed. Last night had been one hell of a ride and today we were going to perform bush surgery on Chaser's arm. Thinking about the logistics only made me squirm. It was going to hurt...*a lot*.

"Hi."

I looked over my shoulder at Wren. "Hey."

"Mind if I join you?"

I shook my head. "Not at all."

The witch came to stand next to me and I looked her over. She appeared human, though she had a scent about her that felt slightly metallic. I wondered if I was picking up on her magic.

"Where's the vampire?"

"Not far."

Chaser had gone into town for supplies, which was a big deal considering he didn't trust Wren's motivations. He'd warned me before he'd left that she might decide her plan was easier and knock me over the head. I trusted her, but after the things I'd been through, there was still a grain of doubt.

"I had a lot of time to think last night," Wren began as she leaned against the railing.

"So did I," I admitted.

"When I came here, I expected you to be like your father. I expected a fight."

I said nothing, waiting to see where she was going.

"Your vampire would've killed me if it wasn't for you." She sighed and lowered her gaze. "I wanted to say... I wanted to say I'm sorry."

At first, I was a little taken aback, but I smiled. "I know it's not the best situation to get to know one another, and we don't really have the time, but I appreciate you helping us with the talisman."

Wren shrugged.

"So...*witches*," I said, sitting in one of the lawn chairs. "What's the deal with that?"

Wren smiled and sat in the chair beside mine, the plastic creaking. "Well, I was born this way. Magic is inherited, though it depends on the bloodline as to what elemental affinity that magic holds."

"Elemental affinity? What's that?"

"Earth, air, fire, water, or spirit," she explained. "Witches can call on all five, but one is always stronger than the rest."

"Oh..." I mulled over it for a moment. "What is your element then?"

"Fire." Wren shrugged and averted her gaze like she was ashamed of it.

"You can manipulate fire? Sounds cool to me...but why do I sense you're not so thrilled about it?"

"There's a...*history* with my bloodline," she admitted. "A bad one."

"Like what?"

"They say it was my ancestor, the beginning of my line, who was responsible for creating all vampires."

I grimaced as I realised why the Hollow Men had taken an interest in her family. King was looking for a way to become truly immortal, so it was no wonder he'd manipulated Wren's coven. If they still had access to the spell that created the first vampire, maybe they had access to more. Considering he was after me, I had a feeling they didn't.

"King manipulated you," I said. "That's nothing to be ashamed about."

"It's not that. She betrayed all witches when she made the vampires. Her blood runs in my veins."

"Blood doesn't mean shit." I waved my arms in the air. "Just look at me. If it was true, then I'd be like Marini. I'd rather choke on my own vomit than be a shred like that man."

Wren sighed. "I like to think that, but sometimes I'm not so sure."

"*C'mon.*" I leaned forwards, the chair creaking dangerously. One of these days, the sun-bleached plastic was going to break completely.

"Just look at what I was going to do to you."

"That has nothing to do with blood," I told her. "The vampires killed your entire family for standing up to them. If I was in your position, I might've done the same thing." I hesitated.

Wren picked up on my uncertainly and snorted. "You don't believe that."

"I do, I just... I killed my father. Tore out his throat. I'm not sure..." I swallowed hard and pushed away the memory. "No one can truly understand until they're in the same position. It's not my place to judge you; I can only forgive." I ran my fingers through my hair. "What I mean to say is that actions speak louder than blood ever will."

"Said by someone who only just found out the supernatural world exists." Wren sank back in her chair and sighed. "Everything is about blood."

Footsteps on the stairs behind us ended our conversation before I could reply, and I narrowed my eyes.

"Don't stop on my account," Chaser said, appearing behind us. "I was riveted."

"Did you get what we need?" Wren asked.

"There wasn't much to choose from at the

supermarket, but I got what I could," he told her. "Which is a knife, a hammer, a handsaw, a chisel, fishing line and hooks."

My mouth fell open as he showed me the contents of the reusable shopping bag.

"You're going to cut open your arm with this?" I exclaimed, holding up a fillet knife. "You're not filleting a barramundi, Chaser."

"It's the best we've got," he said, handing the bag to Wren. He gave her a pointed look. "I'm trusting you. Don't make me regret it."

"We are not doing it on the roof," I exclaimed, jerking to my feet. "It's not sterile for one, and two—"

"I'm a vampire," Chaser interrupted. "I don't need alcohol swabs."

"We can go somewhere in the bush," Wren said, looking through the bag. "It'll be better. I need clear access to my magic and the less barriers between me and the elements, the better."

"It's an outdoorsy thing?" I asked.

"Buildings dampen magic."

Interesting. I made a mental note, wondering if it'd have any impact on the alleged wards on the *Halcyon*.

"Do you have the talisman?" Chaser asked me, and I tapped my shirt pocket. "Then let's get this over with."

―――――――

We found a secluded patch of gum trees half a kilometre from the motel and made ourselves comfortable. It was far enough away from the road to keep us out of sight, and far enough from town where no one would accidentally stumble across us.

I lingered amongst the trees as Chaser and Wren prepared, taking in the flat expanse of farmland. It was a beautiful vista, all green and gold with maturing wheat and blue from the summer sky. Too bad it was about to become the scene of a brutal magical surgery.

"I'll cast spells to help me cut the bone and slow the bleeding," Wren explained as Chaser began to work with the hooks and fishing line. "Things will go faster that way."

I glanced at Chaser, who'd positioned himself on the trunk of a fallen tree. "So, then you just have the position the bone and his vampire healing will do the rest?"

"Yes," he said. "My bone will fuse with the talisman and my flesh will heal."

"Are you sure you want to do this?" I asked. "I mean... It's going to hurt."

He took my hand. "I expect it will."

"Chaser..."

"Anything to keep you safe," he murmured, letting me go.

If Wren had an opinion about our exchange, she kept it to herself.

Chaser straddled the tree and set his arm before him. "Let's begin, shall we?"

Wren took a deep breath and picked up the knife. "Here goes nothing."

I felt like throwing up as I watched her cut into Chaser's flesh. Skin and muscle parted like butter, exposing the pinkish-white bone beneath.

Chaser barely moved, though his forehead creased as he held onto his pain. It must've been excruciating, but he didn't make a sound. I, on the other hand, began to fret as Wren used Chaser's makeshift fishing lure contraption to anchor the wound open.

"I'm going to be sick." I slapped my hand over my mouth.

"Vampires heal fast," Wren said. "I know it looks bad, but if it closes over, I'll just have to cut him open again."

"Just get on with it," Chaser said, grimacing.

Wren picked up the handsaw, but it was too large to cut the bone, so she discarded it in favour of the hammer and chisel.

My expression faded and my breakfast almost made a repeat appearance, but I squashed it down when I saw Chaser's already pale complexion turn an odd shade of bluish-grey.

I knew the witches that Fortitude had used all those decades ago had wiped his memory to conceal the truth about the talisman, but it'd also erased the pain. Reality and memory were two different beasts and right now, Chaser was struggling. Underneath all that bravado and cool vampiric exterior, it was easy to forget that he still felt pain.

I had to be strong for him. *I had to be strong.*

Placing my hands on his shoulders, I pressed against him. "I'm here," I whispered into his ear. "*You can do this.*"

Wren began to chant in a strange language as she called on her magic and the air around us shifted. Amongst the tang of blood, I could pick up on the tendrils of something unknown. It tasted like burning metal, like sparks from a forge, and my eyes widened as Wren raised the chisel.

The tip glowed bright orange, her magic feeding into the tool as she positioned it over the bone in Chaser's arm. His blood had stopped flowing and the field was clear.

I tightened my grip on his shoulders as she struck the hammer. His whole body jerked, but he never made a sound, not even when his arm snapped.

Wren's chanting continued, her magic working to sever the last sliver, then the bone was gone, and she was placing the talisman into the gap.

I didn't have the courage to look as she removed the hooks, but as Chaser's trembling began to subside, I chanced it. His flesh knitted back together, the talisman disappearing underneath muscle, blood, and sinew. Then his skin curled, the edges reaching towards each other. It was mesmerising in a macabre kind of way.

"It's done," Wren said, putting the bloodied tools back inside the bag. "The bone accepted the talisman. You shouldn't have any problems with it."

I cradled Chaser's head in my hands, my heart pounding. "Are you alright?"

"The pain is gone, Sloane," he said. "You can let me go."

I peeled myself away, reluctant to let him out of my grasp. He'd taken the whole thing with unnatural stoicism. Was that a vampire thing or something else? I wasn't sure if he'd ever let me in on the secret, whatever it was.

Chaser stood and eyed the witch. For a moment, neither of us knew what he was going to do, but finally, he held out his hand towards her.

Wren looked at it for a moment, completely bewildered, then took it in her own.

"Thank you," he said. It was as close to an apology for his behaviour as she was going to get.

She raised her eyebrows. "Y-you're welcome."

CHAPTER 8
CHASER

I took inventory of all our belongings that night. It kept my mind off the memory of putting the talisman in my arm.

The pain had been excruciating, but I didn't care. If it kept Sloane safe, then I'd do it again and again. The magic would always be with me, but no one could use it against us ever again...unless they cut it out.

I set out all our things on the table in our motel room and counted. We had two guns—the revolver and my 10mm pistol—and a couple of boxes of ammunition, including some wooden bullets. I always carried cash for the times I couldn't rely on compulsion, so that wasn't a problem. There was one mobile phone between us and both our bags of clothing, which I'd recovered from the tents outside the cottage before we'd left the night of the attack.

Traveling light was good, but we'd need more

supplies before this was over. Sloane would need her own burner phone in case she wanted to go to the supermarket for more snacks.

She sat beside me. "Hey... Um..."

I glanced at her. "What?"

"Are you okay?" She reached out towards my arm but pulled back at the last moment.

"Sloane, I understand you're worried about me, but don't be." I lifted my arm so she could see the unblemished skin on my forearm. "It's completely healed. There's no pain. It was gone the moment it healed over."

"And you're just fine with it?"

I blinked. "Why wouldn't I be?"

"Wren gutted you like a fish and chiselled out your bone. I know you felt every moment of it, and now you're sitting there like it never happened."

I shrugged.

"Shoe's on the other foot now, huh?"

"It's not a competition," I told her. "I just did what had to be done, so stop reading more into it. Some things are just that simple, Sloane."

She studied me for a long moment, then sighed. "I don't think I'll ever understand vampires."

"I've been forced to endure the company of werewolves for a hundred years, and I don't understand them, either."

"There's the Chaser I know and love," she drawled, falling back onto the bed. "I won't ask you again."

I eyed her, the L-word twisting through me like barbed wire. She hadn't realised what she'd said, and I didn't have it in me to enlighten her. Love was still a foreign concept, one that I was afraid of after what'd happed to Loretta, and it was a miracle I even admitted *that* to myself.

Fear was one thing, but love? It was a test I didn't want to take in the current climate. Not when we were about to head into Hollow Men territory. Not when I mightn't leave the city alive.

"Can you hand me the chocolate?" Sloane asked, waving her hand in the air. "I need a sugar rush before I go all ballistic and hormonal on you."

Snorting, I threw the block of Cadbury's Top Deck at her, which landed on her stomach with a smack.

"Ow!" She sat up and glared. "Seriously?"

"*Seriously.*" I'd dodged one missile and replaced it with another. Classic arsehole move. "Don't eat it all in one go. We're going to need it for the drive tomorrow."

***

We checked out of the motel the next morning and loaded our meagre belongings into the car.

I watched Sloane as she said her goodbyes to Wren, who had directions to her safe harbour with Gasket and the pack at the newly-reacquired Fortitude compound. To my surprise, they hugged like friends. A day ago, the witch had come here to kidnap her, and now the pack had a powerful ally rather than another enemy.

I shook my head and sighed. At least she wouldn't be alone.

As Wren got into her car and drove off, I knew it wouldn't be the last time we saw the witch before the end. Until then, we had our own path to follow.

Sloane walked over to me and lifted her bag into the boot of the car, oblivious to my staring.

The real long game was about to begin, yet she seemed too excited for my liking. There was a line between grey and complete darkness—a border I'd become familiar with—and I was starting to worry she was about to cross the point of no return.

Would she face her father's death or would she revel in it?

I used to see her indifference as a sign of strength, but now I wasn't so sure. We were about to head into enemy territory, and if she came apart at the wrong moment, it could mean her life.

"Sloane?"

She looked up, her eyes sparkling. Her sunglasses were on her head, pushing away long, messy tresses of hair from her face.

"What now?" she asked as I slammed the boot closed. "We've talked about everything already."

"I'm not convinced."

She eyeballed me. "About Wren or about your arm?"

"Neither."

She sighed and rolled her eyes. "Are we still on the whole killing my father business?"

"It's not a joke."

"No, it's not. I told you how I feel about it."

"Indifferent?"

She threw her hands into the air. "I don't know what you want me to say."

I didn't know, either.

"If you want, I'll let you do the honours," she added. "That is what it's about, right? You think I'm going to lose my soul by taking out the guy who Marini was going to sell me to as a loaded weapon. Am I right?"

I raised my eyebrows.

"What?" She screwed up her nose. "As long as he's dead, then whatever. You pull the trigger or I pull the trigger," she shrugged, "the result is the same."

"I don't..."

"This is our forever we're talking about," she said. "So get in the car already."

I wrenched open the driver's side door and slid inside, wondering when I'd become such a weakling. Oh yeah, it was when I finally found something worth dying for.

Killing King might send her right over the edge, but maybe that wasn't what I was so worried about. Maybe it was something else...something more sinister.

I ran my thumb over my forearm, tracing the line where Wren had sliced me open, then turned the key in the ignition. Maybe I was still adjusting to my humanity. I *had* gone decades without it.

Sloane clipped on her seatbelt and pointed towards the highway. *"Let's blow this popcorn stand."*

CHAPTER 9
SLOANE

As we drove, the flat plains gradually gave way to lush bushland, and finally the outskirts of the city.

I leaned towards the window, positioning myself in front of the vents, the air flow cooling my flushed skin. Fiddling with the silver ring Wren had given me before she'd gotten in her car, I wondered if werewolves ran hotter than humans. I'd certainly struggled with the heat ever since I'd turned out on the Nullarbor.

"What's that?" Chaser asked, glancing at me.

"A ring. Wren gave it to me," I said absently. "A thank you gift."

"Let me see."

I offered my hand to him, and he studied the twisted silver band and the little piece of polished quartz set in the middle. After a moment, he grunted and fixed his gaze back on the road.

"What?" I asked.

"It has magic on it, you know."

I shrugged. "Cool."

"Did she say what it's for?"

"Nope."

"And you're just going to wear it?"

"*Yep.*" I popped the 'p' at the end and turned back to the road, watching the city emerge out of the smokey haze.

Buildings began to rise and the road gained a border of artificial sound barriers. A fast-food restaurant attached to a service station sailed by, then a densely packed industrial park, and finally, the highway turned into four inbound freeway lanes snaking all the way towards the smudge of skyscrapers in the distance.

We crossed over the West Gate Bridge, the elevation giving me a bird's eye view of the Docklands, then we skirted to the south of the CBD where I got a glimpse of the *Halcyon Casino*.

Chaser merged off the freeway and stopped at a traffic light. Ahead, I could see a billboard—which looked like it was twenty stories high—flashing advertisements for the *Halcyon*.

The lights changed and we moved, coasting through the heart of the city.

I stared out the window, my eyes flicking back and forth, taking everything in. How didn't the throngs of people walking up and down the footpaths see what was just under their noses? Vampires, witches, *werewolves*. How did all that go unnoticed by so many?

"How can't they see?" I asked, glancing at Chaser.

"See what?"

"*Us*. Supernaturals. The Hollow Men sent a car bomb into the compound. There was a firefight at DeLuca's place. How does that kind of stuff fly underneath the radar?"

"Supernaturals have been concealing themselves from humanity for thousands of years," he told me. "It's second nature."

"But *how?*"

"Vampires are ancient, Sloane. They don't just use compulsion. Some have amassed wealth and political influence beyond compare. It's a sport to them."

"Vampires like King?"

Chaser nodded. "Exactly like King."

"It's so..." I couldn't think of a good word to describe it.

"Outlandish?"

"Yeah," I murmured, turning back to the window. *Outlandish to think we had a chance against power like that.*

Outside, Melbourne was in the midst of another busy workday. I wondered how we were meant to surveil anything around here—it was so busy, built up, and there would be tight security at the casino. We were here for one vampire, and I didn't want to accidentally hurt innocent bystanders.

"How are we going to do this?" I asked. "It's so..." I was lost for words again as the enormity of our task was smooshed right into my face.

"With great difficulty."

I settled back into the seat, my sight blurring away from the bustling city.

After we drove a few more blocks, Chaser turned the car down a side street, and we zoomed into a self-parking garage. Artificial lights flicked past as we circled around, looking for a space to park. When we finally found one, Chaser deftly backed into it, then cut the engine.

"Here." He reached over to the backseat and produced an awful black trucker hat with an embroidered kangaroo motif on the front. He put it on my head and tugged the bill down.

"Are you trying to make me look like a bogun?" I asked.

"Like a tourist, but that works, too."

"Hilarious."

"The more we can blend in, the better." He showed me his hat, and I smirked. "Don't even say it."

"I never said a thing," I retorted.

"We need to get you a burner phone when we get a chance," he went on.

"Why?"

"In case we get separated. Then we've got a way to contact one another that won't be traceable."

"No safe words or meeting points?"

Chaser leaned towards me and placed his palm on my thigh. "I don't intend to let you out of my sight if I can help it."

I smiled and caught him in a quick kiss.

"This might go down fast, or we might be waiting a long time," he murmured. "Either way, we have to be ready to get out of the city as quickly as we can."

"We'll be ready." I nodded. "Where will we go?"

"Away."

"Let's go to Tasmania."

"What the hell is in Tasmania?"

"Horses," I replied with a shrug.

"Horses? They have them all over, you know."

"I think the point is that it's *away*."

Chaser raised his eyebrows and put on his trucker hat. Ironically, he looked really good in it.

"Let's go," he said as he opened his door and slid out.

I followed, waiting as he locked up and rounded the bonnet.

"Where are we going to stay?" I asked, shying away as my voice echoed a little too loudly. Luckily, there was no one around.

"We'll do a sweep first, then we'll figure it out."

"A sweep?" I asked as we walked towards the exit. "What does that mean?"

"I want to test the perimeter of the *Halcyon*," he explained. "See where their security begins, where the cameras are, the magical wards, and who's on their payroll outside."

I frowned. This was more complicated than I first realised. I mean, I knew it was going to be hard, but all this...? I wasn't a secret agent with specialised training; I was just a woman with an axe to grind. Chaser was the guy with all the smarts.

"What are Monroe's leads anyway?" I asked. "You never told me."

"Entrances, exits, security rotations," Chaser murmured. "Wards, alarms..."

"And how long since he was in their favour?"

He shrugged. "A while."

I knew time was a different beast for a vampire, and I wrinkled my nose. "I don't like it."

"It's not ideal, but it's all we've got. That's why I want to do a sweep."

"To make sure Monroe isn't full of shit?"

"Yes."

Doubt clouded my mind as we left the parking garage and headed towards the *Halcyon*. Ahead, I could see the world beyond, and I wanted nothing more than to puke in the gutter, then turn around and run.

Chaser tugged me forwards, my boots feeling heavy, then we were on the border between the old and the new. The new wasn't so hot if you asked me.

I glanced up and down the street, watching the flow of foot traffic. There were so many people. My stomach gurgled, and I realised I was nervous. We'd talked, done all the research, prepared for what was coming, and now we were here... I wasn't ready, but I had to be. There was no backing out once I stepped onto the street.

I tensed as Chaser slid his hand into mine. It wasn't like him to be all public display of affection, but knowing he was close made my anxiety settle some.

"This is it," he murmured, leaning in close. "There's still time to turn back."

I lingered on the edge of the footpath, my life flashing before my eyes. Well, it wasn't quite like that, but I thought about all the things that'd brought me here. The multiple times my father had attempted to sell me to King, the attack behind the *Sailor's Arms*, and the incident on the train with Bailey and the fake conductor. My mother's murder, the childhood I'd missed out on, my escape from Fortitude all those years ago, and the future I'd so desperately tried to find. So much had happened that I hardly understood who I'd become.

I knew what I was—the wolf who could change at will—but *who* I was, was still a mystery.

Then there was Chaser. He was in this deeper than I would ever be. The Hollow Men had stolen everything from him, including his human life. The loss had driven Chaser to take matters into his own hands, and as a result, King had killed Loretta right in front of his eyes.

Yeah, Chaser was in this deeper than I would ever be.

Thinking of the things he'd done for me, I knew I couldn't abandon him now. If I backed down, he'd still carry on with the plan, with or without me, and I'd be another person on the list of those who'd betrayed him. I had to stay...for myself, but mostly, for him. That was what love was, right?

I took a deep breath and slid my sunglasses on. "Let's go."

I pulled my trucker hat lower and peered across the square.

The sun was hot as sin, and I leaned a little farther into the shade. Across the flow of tourists, I could see a guy watching the comings and goings, a bulge in the left pocket of his shorts. When he angled to the left, I could see the telltale antenna on a hidden walkie-talkie.

It was just like Chaser had said. Between our hand-to-hand combat training session on the roof of that rundown Mallee motel, and his crash course in spotting security on the five-hour drive, something *had* sunk in, though I made sure to keep my distance from my target. My first time 'sweeping' was working out decently enough, but my stomach still churned.

"Hey."

My heart skipped a beat as Chaser appeared beside me. Sitting on the ledge, he nodded towards the guy I'd been tailing.

"Case him?" he asked, opening a leaflet so I could pretend to look at it with wonder. It was a brochure for the Human Nature residency at the *Halcyon*, and I made a mental note to give him shit about it later.

"Yeah," I replied with a nod.

The thirty-six floors of the *Halcyon Casino* stood above us, daunting in size. Outside, there were various shops and restaurants full with people to near bursting. Neon signs and billboards advertised the theatre shows and shopping inside, all of which were top-dollar entertainment.

I sighed and glanced at the man again. The enemy's doorstep wasn't the optimal place to test out my developing skills, but we didn't have much choice, what with renegade wolves on one side and Hollow Men on the other.

"I've counted four guys in the forecourt," I murmured, pretending to look at the brochure. "But that guy is the laziest. All the others have been real pros."

"Cameras?"

"The place is crawling with them," I replied. "There's two at the side entrance, three at the main, one on the restaurant, and the one behind us is operated by the city."

"Good. I see you were listening."

"I always listen to what you say," I replied, pinching his leg. "I just don't always agree."

Chaser snorted, then folded up the brochure. "C'mon, I got us a room at the hotel across the street."

"Is that a good idea? I mean..." I glanced back at the man and narrowed my eyes. "If you hadn't told me what to look for, I wouldn't have even known."

"I took precautions." He slid his hand into mine, stood, then pulled me to my feet.

I pretended to know what he meant by that, just glad to walk in the opposite direction of the *Halcyon*. The whole place had this...*vibe*, like something wasn't right. I imagined it was the kind of place that tossed cheaters and gamblers with huge debts out the back door, then kicked them three-quarters to death. I sniffed the air, almost believing I could smell the blood.

"What about the wards?" I asked. "How do we know where the magic is?"

Chaser gave me a look and pulled me towards the footpath. "We'll come back tonight."

"Tonight?" I squeaked.

"Sloane, are you sure you can—"

"Yes," I snapped, shutting off the stupid voice inside my head that was feeding my doubts. "*I can.*"

"Good, because tonight we're going inside that hellhole."

I swallowed hard as we crossed the street, making for the hotel opposite.

Inside the Halcyon? I hoped I was ready for that because bravado would not help me face an entire gang of ancient vampires, not one bit.

CHAPTER 10
CHASER

Our hotel room was a nest of silence in the midst of the bustle of central Melbourne.

The room was spacious with a view that overlooked the *Halcyon* across the street, the sheer curtains softening the hard edges of the ominous building. It looked like a spire of hard metal shooting towards the sky, jagged and almost like crystal shards inside a geode of shit.

I emptied our bags and spread out the contents on the bed while Sloane was in the shower, washing off the grit and grime of the heat outside.

I folded our clothes into neat piles, then separated all the other bits and pieces. Picking up Sloane's aviator sunglasses, I was hit with the memory of her demanding five dollars from me at that roadhouse. She'd said, 'Five bucks won't emasculate you.' It wasn't that long ago, but it felt like years had passed.

The bathroom door opened, and Sloane padded out, bringing the damp scent of soap with her.

"What are you doing?" she asked, watching me paw through her belongings.

"Taking inventory."

"You did that last night."

She sat on the bed next to me, her gaze raking over the neat piles of clothes. She didn't say anything about me breaching her privacy, so I figured we were even for the time she went through my stuff on the train.

"We're going to need to leave quickly," I explained. "I want to make sure we have everything we need to disappear. We might not be able to return to the pack at first."

"Oh..." she murmured.

"Here." I pointed to each item and explained what I was tossing and what I was putting in. "We want to keep things light, so anything heavy is out. The hotel toiletries are small, though they're a luxury, but they will tide us over if we need to be on the road longer than a couple of days. Cash is a given. Spare ammo and a gun each. Burner phones." I pointed to the mobile phone I'd assembled for her. "And a change of clothes."

"You stole the amenities box from the bathroom," she declared.

"I didn't steal anything. It's *complimentary*."

Sloane was silent for a moment. "This is going to work, isn't it?"

I'd thought about it over and over, but the conversation I'd had with Monroe and his dead-end leads had solidified it in concrete. It wasn't even worth chasing them to begin with. After a century of hunting wolves and infiltrating rival packs for Fortitude, I knew better than anyone that what Monroe offered was less than actionable. All he'd done was confirm what I'd already suspected—there was no other way in. The *Halcyon* and the Hollow Men, who ruled it, were watertight. Nothing was getting in or out without them knowing about it, and I'd put the old vampire in danger for nothing.

The only thing left to do was knock on the front door. The plan was simple, yet full of uncertainty. Things could go wrong—that was how life went—but there was no other way. I knew this was what I'd have to do the moment I left Monroe's diner.

I just didn't know how to tell Sloane. No matter what she told me, I knew her courage was hanging by a thread. That's why she couldn't know what I was about to do.

"I need to go out," I said. "Stay here."

I stood and picked up the 'do not disturb' hanger for the door.

Sloane rose to her feet. "Where are you going?"

"Just to the foyer. I won't be long."

"Why?"

I ignored her, knowing I was going to pay for it later, and left.

The *Halcyon* towered above me, glittering like a steaming turd rolled in glitz and glamour.

What I was about to do was insane, but I had to walk in and demand a meeting with King. I couldn't stand before him without anything to offer, so I'd have to sell Sloane out...but I also had to want something in return. It meant I had to tell him the truth about my forced slavery and demand his legion of witches free me from the magic binding me to the werewolves. The wolf for my freedom, or so the ruse went.

There was no other way.

Taking out my phone, I dialled Sloane's burner.

She answered in one ring. "Chaser...?"

"Whatever you do, don't leave the room."

"What are you talking about?" she demanded. "Where are you?"

"I'm about to walk into the *Halcyon* and end all your troubles."

The line rustled. "You can't be serious!"

"This is the only way," I told her. "Monroe's information is useless. It will never get us close to King, but if I go in there and demand a meeting, I'll be face-to-face with the bastard."

"*No.* No, you can't, Chaser," she said, but her voice wavered.

"Don't lose your nerve now," I murmured. "After all we've been through, I know I can do this."

She was silent for a few minutes, though I could hear her ragged breathing on the other end of the line.

"You want to sell me out to infiltrate the Hollow Men?"

"I see we think alike."

"I can't..." She took a deep breath. "I promised you forever, Chaser. This isn't forever. So many things could go wrong."

"I don't intend to die, Sloane."

"*That's good*, but tell that to the casino full of vampires."

"We both know the stakes," I told her, looking up at the tower. "If we want forever, free and clear, we have to end this as soon as possible."

"Now or never?"

"The deeper we get, the tougher it is to get out."

"You don't have to tell me that. My whole life has been devoted to getting out."

"Sloane..." I took a deep breath and wished I'd kissed her one last time. "I don't want you to get any deeper into this."

"That's not your choice to make," she snapped. "You left without so much as a word. The moment you stand before King and kill him is the moment they turn around and *kill you*. They'll never let you leave."

"That's a risk I'm willing to take."

"But *I'm not*. This is no better than the plan Marini had."

"It is, Sloane. In this plan, only one of us is in danger and death is not a certainty. Don't forget, I'm still bound by the talisman. They can kill me, but I'll just come back."

"And so will the Hollow Men," she hissed. "King is just one vampire. Another will step up and take his place."

"You're forgetting something else, Sloane," I drawled, taking a step towards the *Halcyon.* "I was one of them. King is the glue that binds the entire organisation together. Without him, it all falls apart."

"It sounds like you've put a lot of thought into this. *When did you get the time?*"

My mood darkened. "Do you want forever, Sloane? Or for now?"

"Forever," she snapped. "Always forever."

"Then this is the plan."

"Chaser—"

I hung up, fired off a quick text, then turned the phone off and slipped it into my pocket. There was no turning back now.

Walking through the crowd, I entered the casino and glanced up at the security cameras as I passed beneath them.

Behind me, I knew Sloane was looking out the hotel window, trying to spot me in the stream of humans out for a good night...but she never would.

This is for your forever, Sloane. Don't forget it.

I walked across the gaming floor, passing blackjack

tables and spinning roulette wheels, reciting my mantra in my mind.

Freedom, love, forever...

Every so often, I spotted a plant—vampires with concealed weapons and walkie-talkies, and even the odd woman draped in glitzy fabric encouraging gamblers to put down more money with a flourish of vampiric compulsion.

I was surprised no one had stopped me. I aimed for the hotel beyond the gaming floor, where I'd approach the elevator and press the button for the penthouse.

Passing a row of slot machines, I saw a man speak into a walkie-talkie, his gaze following me. I'd been made. *Took them long enough.*

Increasing my stride, I spotted the hotel entrance.

"Stay right where you are."

Turning, I saw a male vampire aiming a gun at me. Movement to my left caught my attention, and I glanced at another man who'd pulled another gun. The same happened on my right and behind, until six drawn weapons surrounded me.

"Don't move, Mason," a familiar voice barked.

I snorted and looked over my shoulder at Holden, another Englishman who'd been turned by King around the same time as I had. He hadn't changed, apart from his choice in clothing, but vampires rarely did. He was still the same stocky, hard-faced, shaved-headed bruiser I'd met in the first days with the Hollow Men.

"You shouldn't have come back here," he said, stepping in-between the row of guns.

"I want to see him," I snarled. "I want to see King."

My arms were wrenched behind me. Someone patted me down as a pair of handcuffs were slapped around my wrists, the metal biting painfully into my skin. I felt the magic grab hold of my vampirism and squeeze the strength out of me, but it didn't seem to dampen the power radiating from the talisman.

"It's been a hundred years," Holden said. "You should have let her go."

The casino swarmed around us, the noise fading to a dull roar.

"This isn't about her..." I drawled. "*It's about the wolf.*"

The line cut out and I cursed. *Chaser, you damn fool!*

I stood and began to pace as the phone dinged with a text message. Snatching it up, I cursed again as I read what Chaser had sent.

If I'm not back by sunrise, go find Gasket.

I tried to call him back but the line wouldn't connect, and I hurled the phone into my bag with a cry of frustration.

If they figured out Chaser was lying, they'd kill him—the talisman wasn't the same as true immortality. He could still die permanently...or they could use him as bait to lure me out.

So many things could go wrong and only one thing could go right. I didn't like those odds.

I fisted my hands into my hair and tugged. What was I going to do?

I snorted and rolled my eyes, already knowing there was only one thing I could do. *Go after him.*

When the Hollow Men caught him—because it was now when, not if—they would follow his trail here. It meant I had to go against what he thought was right and leave. *Now.*

Remembering what he'd told me about having to make a run for it, I pulled his belongings out of his bag and stuffed them into mine.

Travel light. Only take what was necessary. I couldn't carry two bags, one was enough.

I didn't understand how vampires tracked, let alone what spells witches used, so I pulled everything I could out of the bathroom—even scraped the bin clean—and balled it up into the used towels and shoved it into Chaser's empty bag.

Legging it out of the room, I shouldered my bag and scanned for somewhere I could dump his that didn't look suspicious. I rode the elevator to the foyer, edging into the corner as a group of people got on. I sniffed, but I couldn't smell anything besides perfume and cologne. Humans.

When the doors slid open, I let them get off first, and scanned the comings and goings, but I couldn't sense anything supernatural in the air.

It'd been three minutes since I got Chaser's text. I had to hurry.

Putting my head down, I took the side entrance, skirting around the restaurant and out into a lane. A row of dumpsters sat against the wall, and I flung Chaser's bag into the first one and kept walking until I reached the road.

The *Halcyon* looked even more terrifying in the dark. It was lit up with artificial lighting that would burn human retinas, let alone supernatural ones, but there was still that air of sinister terror I'd felt that afternoon.

Courage in pain and adversity, I though, using Fortitude's motto to drive me forwards.

Keeping my head down, I entered the casino.

I crossed the gaming floor, spotting several vampires as I went, but none of them saw me.

I looked around, trying to spot Chaser, homing in on a commotion in the direction of the *Halcyon* hotel.

I stopped by a row of noisy slot machines—otherwise known as *pokies*—and my heart stopped beating.

I saw six vampires surrounding Chaser with their guns drawn and knew there was nothing I could do. I stood and didn't even lift a finger. I couldn't.

I stood behind the bank of pokies as people on the casino floor walked past the group without even slowing. It was as if they were invisible. The humans couldn't see the truth of this place and now, I was beginning to understand why the Hollow Men could get away with so much. Compulsion, magic...it was one big web of lies.

I watched they put handcuffs around Chaser's

wrists and a vampire with a shaved head said something to him. Even with my enhanced hearing, I couldn't hear them over the noise of the casino. Then they dragged him towards the hotel entrance, the people milling about oblivious to what was happening.

My heart twisted and a wave of nausea caused my skin to heat. *Chaser…*

I kept my head down and left the *Halcyon*, trying to think of a plan. There was no way this plan was going off without a hitch. I hadn't met the arsehole, but King was too smart for that. He struck me as the kind of guy who'd thought of every angle, every point of attack, even the one's Chaser wouldn't have considered.

As I stepped out into the warm evening, with the Melbourne nightlife bustling around me, I realised Chaser had just sacrificed himself for me. He knew he was going to die. *He knew.*

He was such a bloody idiot.

CHAPTER 12

SLOANE

I walked away from the *Halcyon*, my entire body trembling.

They hadn't even seen me—not once glance, not one shout of alarm. *Nothing.* The most wanted wolf in the whole country had slipped into the enemy's lair without so much as a twitch. It was as if I were invisible.

I twisted the ring Wren had given me around my finger and wondered... Chaser had said there was magic on it. Had it concealed me from the Hollow Men and the wards their witches had cast on the casino? It had to have. There was no other reason why I walked in and out without being noticed.

That's it!

Magic.

If I had any hope of getting Chaser out of the *Halcyon*, I needed Wren.

I sat on a bench by the Yarra River and took out the burner phone Chaser had left me. Hoping the witch had found Gasket, I dialled his number, the line connecting almost instantaneously.

"Yeah?" came his gruff voice.

"It's Sloane. I need to talk to Wren."

"Hello to you, too."

A tram rumbled past, the driver ringing the bell furiously at a slow-moving pedestrian. I turned away from the street, ducking into an alcove. "Gasket, I'm kind of on the clock here."

"Wait." He paused. "Was that a tram? Where are you?"

"In the city," I told him. "Look—"

"In the *city*? Sloane, are you mad? The Hollow Men are still after you, and if you hadn't noticed, we've still got renegade wolves out there. If they find you, it's over."

"They won't find me," I snapped, hoping I was right about Wren's ring. "You worry about the renegades, Gasket. The Hollow Men are up to me and Chaser."

"And where is our token vampire? Usually by now, he's taken the phone off you."

"Chaser's done something stupid, and I need Wren's help getting him out of it. Is she there or not?"

"Sloane, I know you and Chaser have a thing, but—"

"*Is she there or not?*"

Gasket sighed. "Hang on."

She'd made it, after all.

The phone rustled and I sank into my hair as I waited, my gaze flickering to the *Halcyon* and the stream of humans walking past.

"Sloane? What's wrong?"

"I need your help," I replied. "Can you meet me?"

"I suppose..." Wren's hesitation was unmistakeable. "What's wrong?"

"There's a situation..." I began, not knowing how much I should tell her. If she knew I planned to infiltrate the casino, she mightn't come. "Chaser and I were separated."

"Oh, I guess I can help you find him, but if you're in the city—"

"Flinders Street," I interrupted. "Across the river by the aquarium. I'll be waiting in Chaser's car. You know the one."

Hanging up before she could respond, I glanced over my shoulder at the *Halcyon* and swallowed the terror rising in my stomach. A few months ago, I was just a nobody working in a pub on the opposite side of the country. Now I was planning a smash-and-grab inside a luxury casino and resort run by vampires.

Courage.

I put my head down and made my way through the crowd of humans, headed for the parking garage where Chaser had left the car.

I was going to need it.

I slouched in the driver's seat of Chaser's car, watching the comings and goings on the footpath ahead. Somewhere in that towering building made of rotten glitz and glamour, was Chaser.

What were they doing to him? Was he standing before King like he'd planned? What were they talking about? Had Chaser killed him? *Was he dead?* My head buzzed with a million and one scenarios, none of them good.

When the passenger door opened, I jerked upright, only relaxing when I saw it was Wren.

"Loitering in vampire territory," she said, following my gaze. "Risky."

I held up my hand, showing her the ring. "Care to explain?"

"About?"

"Wren, I'm not an idiot," I snapped, glaring at her. "I went into the *Halcyon*, and they didn't see me."

Her cheeks paled. "You went inside?"

"No one gave a shit. No alarms went off, no vampires descended to sacrifice me in a blood ritual, no witches flew down out of the air conditioning ducts. *Nothing happened.*"

"The crystal carried a small protection spell," she said with a sigh. "It will shield you from the sight of those who'd do you harm...but it comes with a catch."

"Of course, it does," I drawled.

"Sloane, this is important." She reached out to grasp my arm, but I pulled away. "It will hide you, but only if they don't expect you. That's why you called me here, right? You want to get inside." Wren shook her head. "My answer is no."

"They have Chaser," I hissed, thumping my hands against the steering wheel. "He went in there to kill King, knowing he'd die."

"The talisman will protect him. I know it's magic, Sloane. While he's bound to it, he can't die."

"You and I both know King has a legion of witches who will be able to tell he has that thing in his arm. Unless by some miracle they miss it, he'll die for good this time. If immortality was that easy, King would have his own magical arsehole and leave me alone!"

Wren stared at me, her expression fading from stubborn refusal to unreserved shock.

"You love him," she whispered, looking me over. "I thought you two were just sleeping together." She sighed but the joke was on her—Chaser and I hadn't gone that far. "A wolf loves a vampire..."

"So what?" I barked. "Who cares who loves who? *Who cares?* Isn't there anything you can do? I can't let him do this for me, Wren. I never asked for him to die for me. I never asked anyone—" I let my head fall into my hands. "*I never asked...*"

Wren pulled in a deep breath, her gaze moving to the *Halcyon*. "I... I can scry for him."

"Scry?" I lifted my gaze. "What's that?"

"I can use your connection with him to find his location. If he's still alive, we'll get a hit."

My hope took a hit. "And if he's dead...?"

"Don't think like that. Not yet."

"But it's just his location." I shook my head. "It's not enough."

"It's better than nothing." Wren wriggled in the seat, making herself comfortable. "Usually, this kind of spell is done with a map and other amplifying objects, but we're going to have to improvise." She took my hand and closed her eyes, her touch crackling against my skin.

"Amplifying objects?"

"*Shh*." She began to mumble under her breath, chanting as she focused her magic. "He's close..." Her forehead wrinkled. "And his presence is dull...which means he's in there."

"Dull? Because of the magic in the casino?"

Wren nodded and let go of my hand.

"And that's it?" I demanded.

"There's nothing else I can do. Not while he's in the *Halcyon*. There's too much magic and too many vampires."

I hissed and turned away from her. Either she couldn't help me or she was too scared to. In any case, it didn't matter which. I wasn't going to let Chaser die at the hands of the Hollow Men.

"If the ring conceals me from those arsewipes in their fancy casino, then I'm going in there and getting

Chaser out.” I pulled the car keys out of the ignition. “And I’ll tear King’s head off for bonus points.”

“Sloane, that’s not how it works,” Wren argued. “The magic renders you negligible, not invisible. It’ll only get you so far. It’s not a magic bullet for all your problems.”

I shook my head, determined to do whatever it took. Chaser had risked everything for me—not just now, but all along. If I wanted to be his equal, then I had to be prepared to do the same for him, no matter the cost.

“I know you want to go back in there, but it’s a suicide mission,” Wren continued. “I know you have a thing for your vampire, but if you go in there, you’ll be giving them exactly what they want.”

“Chaser,” I said. “His name is *Chaser*.”

“You can’t fight them on your own, and not with just that ring. Sloane, *please*.”

“I don’t care,” I said, opening the door. “As long as it gets me far enough.”

“*Wait*.” Wren grabbed my arm and pulled me back into the car.

“You can’t stop me,” I hissed. “Wren—” The words died in my throat when I saw the glazed look in her eyes and my anger melted away. “Wren?”

The witch blinked and shook her head. “He’s moving.”

“What? How do you know?”

“Drive,” she said, pointing down the street. “*Now*.”

CHAPTER 13
CHASER

I was pulled into an elevator and a black bag was forced over my head.

The material rubbed against my nose and no matter how much I squinted, I couldn't make out anything through the weave. The handcuffs dampened my hearing and ambient noises were difficult to distinguish.

The vampires never uttered another word to me. I was dragged out of the elevator, not knowing if we'd gone up or down. It wasn't until I was forced to sit that they took off the bag off my head.

I blinked at the sudden rush of light, the stark metallic room reflecting the harsh coolness from the artificial bulbs.

Holden glared down at me and handcuffed me to a bar set into the metal table—the chair *and* table were bolted to the floor and reinforced with magic—then left me in silence for what felt like hours. A mirror hung on the opposite wall, reflecting my pathetic appearance. It was definitely a two-way mirror, and I wasn't naïve enough to think I was totally alone.

I shivered, my wrists aching from where the handcuffs were chafing against my skin. They wanted me to break, to allow my thoughts to run so wild that I'd talk myself out of whatever I was planning. I knew what the Hollow Men could do to me. A hundred years was a long time, but the ages never changed the reality of torture.

I didn't know how much time had passed when the door finally opened.

A vampire strode in, his suit and slightly disheveled appearance making him the cliched image of a detective—and maybe he was in his mind-controlled spare time. He carried a manila folder under one arm, the colour bright against his navy suit.

He slid into the chair across the table and leaned back, regarding me with a closed expression. His eyes gave nothing away, but he made it crystal-clear he was the one with the power and I had nothing, not even my strength.

"We've been watching you for a long time, Chaser," the vampire said, opening the file. "A long time."

"Who are you?"

"You can call me Sloss." He flicked through the papers inside the file, not meeting my gaze.

"I came here to see King," I said.

He looked up. "We know."

"And?"

"Understand this, Chaser." Sloss leaned forwards, spreading the contents of the file across the metal tabletop. "You have no power here."

I stared at the photographs, attempting to keep my expression passive. I recognised every single one.

The *Sailor's Arms*. Sloane's apartment in Perth. The roadhouse where the Hollow Men tried to shoot me out back. The charred remains of the vampire bonfire we'd had on the Nullarbor. The wrecked cars on the back roads in South Australia. The train station. The car bomb at the Fortitude compound. The burnt-out shell of DeLuca's cottage.

I looked up at Sloss and he raised his eyebrows, expecting an answer. I didn't have one for him—not one he'd like, anyway.

Sloss was right. I had no power here.

I wondered what Sloane was doing. Hopefully, she'd gotten out of that hotel and called Gasket. They needed to do a scrub for renegades in the remaining crew, but the more King talked, the more I was torn between it being a mole within the pack or if it was just unsubstantiated evidence from Rocket or one of his renegade mates. If they were teaming up with the Hollow Men, it was bad for all of us, especially Sloane.

Sloss stared at me, clearly frustrated with my silence. "The sooner you talk, the easier this will be."

"I don't do easy," I told him. "You'd better just get on with the torture."

"Oh no, we're not there yet," he said. "When I'm done with you, you'll beg me to draw blood."

I frowned, not understanding.

Sloss smirked and undid the top button of his shirt. "Shall we begin?"

A knock at the door elicited a sharp sigh from the vampire and he stood, the chair scraping against the floor. Flashing me one last glare, he strode over and left, leaving me with the photographs.

I tugged at the handcuffs, the magic crackling as I tried to use my strength. It was useless. I wasn't getting out of them until someone undid them.

I knew I'd made a mistake the moment Holden had put them on me. I thought I was doing the right thing, that King wanted Sloane so badly, he would see me in his penthouse, his desperation for true immortality opening a chink in his impenetrable armour. I was counting on it, but my chance was fading. Soon, it would be gone entirely, and Sloane would be alone.

Not alone, I thought. *She'd have Gasket and the pack.*

My gaze flew to the door as it opened, but instead of Sloss, another vampire walked in.

King.

He wore a sharp, tailored suit—black with a subtle grey pinstripe, matching shirt, and silk tie. His silver-streaked hair was swept back in a fancy quiff, and a short-clipped, neat beard gave a rough edge to his refined appearance. When his gaze met mine, there was nothing there. No light, no anger, no happiness... just *nothing*.

As he folded himself into the chair that Sloss had occupied earlier, he unbuttoned his suit jacket with practiced flair. This was a man who loved refinement, revelled in class and intellectual manipulation.

Reaching inside the left breast, he retrieved a handgun he had holstered underneath and placed it on the metal table.

"I know what you did," he said. "That's the only reason I'm talking to you now. The *only* reason."

"And what did I do?"

"Don't play coy with me, William," King said. "While Sloss's talents are unique and riveting to watch, I'd much rather hear the truth come out of your mouth myself. You cannot deny what you've been up to this past century." He shook his head and clicked his tongue, his cool gaze staring right through me. "Werewolves? Didn't you respect anything I taught you?"

I glared, the force of my anger pulling at my dampened vampirism.

"You were always intelligent, William," King drawled. "What happened to you?"

"You happened to me," I snarled.

"Yes! I did, didn't I?" King leaned back in his chair. "Tell me...where is the wolf?"

Damnit. My only chance was to make him an offer

he couldn't refuse. I had to stick to the plan. I had to give him Sloane on a silver platter and hope he'd trust me enough to let me go. The moment I was free, I'd strike.

"That's why I came," I rasped, knowing I looked pathetic. "I'm not with the wolves by choice."

"Interesting..." King waved a hand at me. "Continue."

"I went to them for help, but instead, they bound me to the pack with magic. They forced me into slavery." I gritted my teeth. "I want your witches to free me in exchange for the wolf."

"No," he said, his smile widening. He picked up a photograph, the one with Sloane and me at the roadhouse, and studied it. "You'd never give her up. Just like you never gave up Loretta. At least this time you chose someone more...*durable*."

I jerked against the handcuffs, but they didn't budge. The metal just tore into my flesh, drawing a fresh pulse of blood.

King continued to smile as the metallic scent filled the tiny room. "The witches the Fortitude alpha used to bind you to the pack suffered; I made sure of it. Then I sat back and watched you squirm for a hundred years, knowing that sooner or later, the wolf I was searching for would be born into their pack...and you'd be there to deliver them to me." He chuckled and flung the photograph back onto the table. "I'm a thousand years old, William. I've learned the virtue of patience...and forward planning."

"I don't believe you."

"You didn't think I knew all about Anthony Marini and his little traitor witch Wren? How he planned to link the bloodlines using his daughter and his vampire slave? Thank you for taking care of that for me, by the way. He was the worst alpha that pack ever had."

The truth stabbed into me like a jagged piece of metal, tearing through my chest and piercing my heart. It was a setup from the beginning. Everything I'd done, everything I'd suffered, was for nothing.

"You'll never take her," I snarled. "You think you have it all worked out, and you have...but you're missing one thing."

King narrowed his eyes. "Oh, do enlighten me, William."

"You didn't count on it being *her*," I rasped, my lips quirking. There was no way he could know about our latest movements. How she was across the street in another hotel waiting to strike. When I didn't come back and King was still breathing, Sloane would do everything in her power to end him. "She'll take your plans and *shit all over them*."

I expected King to fly into a rage, to show some sliver of anger, but all he did was laugh. The sound was odd as it stabbed into my chest, maniacal and devoid of humour. *Cold.*

"I suppose you're wondering, what now?" he asked, ignoring my useless shred of defiance.

My jaw tensed.

"As I see it, you're out of options." He leaned back in the chair, looking cool, calm, and collected—the mark of a true psychopath. "Sloane is sitting at the hotel across the street—room 104—waiting for you to return...but of course, you never will. When that door opens, I will be on the other side. *She will be mine.*"

I pulled against the handcuffs again, my vision filling with the haze of uncontrollable rage.

"And now," King stood, doing up the button on his suit jacket, "you will die, knowing there's nothing you can do to save her...just like there was nothing you could've done to save Loretta."

"*Bastard.*"

King raised the gun and pressed it against my chest, aiming directly for my heart.

Then he fired.

CHAPTER 14

SLOANE

I wasn't in a position to argue with Wren, so when she said drive, I drove it like I stole it.

Shoving the key into the ignition, I brought the car to life. The engine roared as I peeled out of the parking spot, horns blaring as I cut off the line of steady traffic.

"Which way?" I asked.

She pointed to the right. "Across the bridge."

I cut across the intersection, sneaking through on an amber light, and we hurtled across the Yarra towards the *Halcyon*.

"The next left," Wren said, her hands plastered to the dashboard.

Scanning the street ahead, I looked for the next turn. It was concealed at the end of the glitzy entrance to the casino, and as I turned the wheel, I realised it was a service road. We passed roller doors and dumpsters before inching underground.

"Are you sure this is right?" I asked, my heart pounding in my chest.

"Yeah." Wren leaned forwards and gestured for me to pull off to the side. "They must be taking him out a service entrance."

As we descended into the shadows, I flipped off the auto headlights before they turned on. I then found an empty loading zone, edged us into it, and killed the engine.

Ahead, a roller door clattered open, the ribbed metal rising slowly. Light poured from within, revealing two men and a gurney.

"Is that...?" I trailed off as I realised they were wheeling out a dark, lumpy, person-shaped bag.

"That's him," Wren said. She was staring at a white transit van as one of the men opened the back.

I swallowed hard. "In the body bag? *Bloody hell.*"

"Don't worry. The talisman's magic is still active. I can feel it from here."

"How?" I asked, worried that the Hollow Men had figured it out and were using it to trap us.

"Because I held it," Wren explained. "I became attuned it its signature when I put it back inside Chaser's arm."

"Can anyone else sense it?"

She shook her head as the two men, who I assumed were vampires, closed the rear doors of the van and circled around to the sides. There was a *thunk* that echoed off the close concrete as they climbed inside. A moment later, the brake lights lit up red.

"Follow at a distance," Wren murmured.

"What if we lose them?"

"We won't."

I turned my head to the side as the van did a U-turn and the headlights flashed across the front of our car. When they didn't slow, I heaved a sigh of relief.

Wren didn't have to direct me. I turned the key in the ignition and the car started, the engine loud in the enclosed space. Then I turned the wheel, doing a sharp U-turn, and followed the van back towards the main road.

My enhanced werewolf vision came in handy as the transit slipped into heavy midday traffic and merged onto the West Gate Freeway.

"Where are they taking him?" I wondered out loud.

Wren shrugged. "To dispose of the body, probably."

I didn't want to think about that, so I narrowed my eyes and watched the van instead.

The transit took the first exit across the bridge, then turned south at the traffic light. We followed at a distance, and when I lost sight of it in a built-up industrial estate, Wren guided me until I caught a flash of white turning into a driveway ahead.

I eased the car off the street and read the sign wired to the fence beside the gate. *Westside Meat Processing.*

"*Holy shit.*" My eyes widened as I realised how the Hollow Men got rid of supernatural bodies. I reached over and wrenched open the glove box, taking out Chaser's 1omm gun. "We've got to get him out."

"Go," she said, opening the passenger side door. "I've got your back."

There was no time to think about what we were doing. It was a snatch and grab, a kill or be killed scenario, a hastily thought-out ambush. But if we did nothing, they'd turn Chaser into mincemeat. *Literally*.

I followed Wren across the nature strip and through the gates, holding the gun in front of me.

"You have to be quick," she murmured. "I won't be able to hold them for long."

I didn't know what she was going to do, but I nodded. "Got it." I was in this now, and I had to commit.

Wren strode towards the van, crossing the concreted yard outside the factory, and raised her hands, her palms facing upwards. She began to chant, speaking in the strange language I'd come to understand was linked to her magic.

The two vampires turned, but before they could react, they clutched their heads and fell to their knees, writhing in agony.

I didn't hesitate. I ran towards the van and unzipped the body bag, gasping when I saw Chaser's desiccated face. His grey skin and withered veins looked much worse than when I'd seen him on the train. He'd come back then, but now he was well and truly dead. It wasn't a good feeling, seeing him like this. It felt so...*final.*

"Sloane!"

Wren's cry brought me back and I turned as a pair of hands grabbed the back of my jacket. I cried out as I was hurled across the yard, rolling across the concrete and jarring my shoulders.

The gun flew from my hand and skidded away. Ignoring the pain, I pushed to my feet and lunged, knowing I had a fifty-fifty chance of grabbing it before he did.

I felt my muscles coil as my inner wolf snarled, pushing me forwards with unnatural speed. Unused to the new sensation, I almost stumbled, but my fingers curled around the grip. I spun, the vampire looming over me, and I opened fire. The bullet ripped through his chest, splattering blood as he staggered. He grunted in pain, his black eyes fixing on me. Baring his fangs, he rushed towards me, but I was already squeezing my finger around the trigger.

This time, the wooden bullet found its mark.

The vampire's eyes widened, then he stumbled, his skin sinking in on itself. He gasped, then collapsed, all grey and wrinkly, but I didn't stop to gloat. I ran towards the transit, looking for Wren.

"Wren?" I cried, pointing the gun out in front of me. "*Wren?*"

Rounding the side of the transit, I saw the gurney

had tipped over, spilling the bag on the ground, then I saw Wren.

She was kneeling on the ground, her eyes wide. The vampire laid dead before her, a gaping hole in his chest where his heart used to be...and beside her was Chaser, his skin sickly grey and his breath ragged.

"Chaser?" My voice sounded child-like, and my heartbeat sped up.

"You came," he rasped, crumpling to his knees on the concrete.

"Of course," I replied, lowering the gun and rushing to his side. "We've had a hell of a day."

"Are you okay? Did they..."

"No." I shook my head. "I'm okay."

He ran his gnarled hands over my body, checking to see if I was all in one piece. "The hotel?"

"What about it?"

"They told me they knew you were there..."

"You know me. I don't like doing what I'm told." I bit my bottom lip, realising how close I'd come to being caught. I turned to Wren and helped her up. "Are you okay?"

She nodded and glanced at the vampire. "It was a close call."

"We need to get out of here," I said, helping Chaser up. "Wren, can you...?"

The witch slunk underneath Chaser's other arm, supporting his weight as we dragged him towards the car.

"What about the bodies?" Wren asked.

Chaser leaned against the car as I unlocked the door, looking sick. "Leave them," he rasped. "The Hollow Men can deal with it."

"But they'll know it was us," I said.

"They'll know anyway," Wren told me as she opened the door.

I nodded as I looked at Chaser. We had bigger problems right now, the first of which was blood.

"We've got a few minutes," I said. "You need blood now, and we can't afford to stop." I thrust my wrist towards him and he balked, shaking his head. "Stop being so high and mighty and drink already." I wriggled my arm. "*Hurry up.*"

Chaser grasped my wrist and frowned. I knew it made him uncomfortable, but he needed to stop looking at me like I was breakable. I was a werewolf now...and I'd finally levelled up. Wren and I had faced those vampires and not pissed our pants. Chaser needed to stop thinking of me as someone who needed to be saved—we could save each other.

As Chaser's fangs sank into my flesh, Wren turned and scanned the street, giving us some privacy. The factory was quiet, the gunshots seemingly passed unnoticed. It *was* an industrial estate, prone to loud bangs. Maybe we'd gotten lucky.

"Don't stop short this time," I murmured as I felt the blood leave my veins.

His gaze flickered to mine, but he didn't stop. The

colour finally returned to his skin and his eyes regained their spark, and he didn't pull away until the greyness had gone completely.

"Are you sure you have enough?" I asked, rubbing my thumb over the wound he'd left behind. It began to heal, tickling as my skin knitted together.

"Enough to get us out of here."

I smirked, glad to have him back. "I hope you're not telling a big, fat porkie pie."

"Sloane. Are you really fine?" He grasped my shoulders and studied me. He had the same look in his eyes when he'd asked me about killing Marini.

"I guess I'm indifferent as always," I murmured.

"What now?" Wren asked, turning now that we were moving again. "We can't stay here."

"We're getting out of the city," Chaser replied, opening the driver's side door.

"We're leaving?" I exclaimed. "*Why?*"

"Why? You're really asking me that after I almost got turned into mince?" Chaser glanced at Wren, then turned to face me. "They knew everything, Sloane. They knew about you, about Marini's plan, about the fire at DeLuca's cottage...*all of it*. I'd say it's a safe bet they're in contact with the renegades."

"With Rocket," I hissed.

He turned around and eyeballed Wren. "He knows all about you, too."

The witch swore under her breath. "I guess you're stuck with me now."

"Wait," I said, grabbing Chaser's arm. "He? You mean King?"

"Yes," he said. "But it's not the time or place to talk about it. This whole city is crawling with Hollow Men. They've got vampires in the police, in local government, and that whole casino is crawling with them. King's operation runs too deep." He grimaced and shook his head. "My plan was never going to work."

I knew how difficult it was for Chaser to admit he'd made a mistake, so even though I wanted to rip him a new arsehole for leaving me like he did, I said nothing.

"Are you sure you can drive?" I asked, narrowing my eyes.

"Get in the car," he barked, sliding inside.

I glanced at Wren, who promptly got it in the back, which left me with the front passenger seat.

Getting in, I shoved my blue aviator sunglasses onto my face with a sigh. Bright lights did nothing for my retinas, but it also hid my annoyance from Chaser. He'd just died and come back to life—*again*—and still, he wouldn't let me drive.

A minute later, we were skirting through the back streets of Altona, the mincemeat factory nothing but a speck behind us.

"First things first," Chaser said, glancing at Wren in the rearview mirror. "We get out of the city. Once they realise I'm gone and their men are dead, they'll come looking for us. Are you in?"

"I have to be," the witch told him. "King knows I'm helping you now. I'm better off with you and your werewolf friends."

"We have to warn Gasket," I said. I knew the pack was trying to reclaim the compound, so it was safe to say the Hollow Men would look for us there first. It would be a slaughter.

"What happened to our bags?" Chaser asked.

"I cleaned out the hotel room before I left," I replied. "I put the used towels and rubbish into your bag, and everything else that smelt like us, then I dumped it inside a bin out the back of the hotel. I put the rest of your stuff into mine. It's in the boot."

Chaser smiled and placed a hand on my thigh, giving me a squeeze. I guess I'd just gotten his version of a gold star.

"So, you're giving up on King?" Wren asked.

Chaser glanced at her in the mirror. "Of course not. I want to see his corpse as much as ever...even more now that he just killed me."

"I have so many questions," I muttered. "*So many.*"

Thinking about all the mistakes we'd made, I wondered if we'd ever get a break. I sighed and rubbed my eyes.

"Tired?" Chaser asked.

"Yeah. I feel like I'm dead on my feet."

"We'll find a place outside of the city. I'll drive for now."

"Is that code for 'sit back and relax'?"

"Sure."

"You're getting soft, you know."

He grunted, his shoulders tensing.

Maybe this was some of the old Chaser showing through—William Mason. The cold, arsehole-ish killer was a product of circumstance, so it stood to reason it wasn't who he really was at his core. If we ever found a place at the end of this where we could be together, perhaps he'd settle into a meshed paring of his two identities.

Maybe was such a hopeless word.

Leaning forwards, I peered into the side mirror, watching the traffic behind us, where I spotted a black SUV. When we turned, it turned. After a few blocks and a set of traffic lights, it was still there. It was a few car lengths away, but it was suspicious enough for me to swallow my fear and tell Chaser.

"I think someone's following us," I said, settling back into the passenger seat.

"I know," Chaser said as Wren turned around.

"You know?" I scoffed and rolled my eyes. "Next time you have a grand plan, don't tell me about it. Oh, wait. *You already did.*"

"This isn't the time, Sloane."

"Neither is thirty minutes before you leave me to walk inside a casino and offer yourself on a silver platter!"

"*Sloane*," he barked. "Let's fight about this later. I don't know who is tailing us, but we need to lose them before we leave the city or we'll never shake them."

"Is this what it's like to be you?" Wren's eyes widened and she checked her seatbelt.

I sighed and offered her an apologetic smile. "If it's any consolation, I'm tired of this shit, too." I tightened my seatbelt as Chaser gunned the engine. "*Real* tired."

CHAPTER 15

SLOANE

C haser glanced in the mirror, and his jaw tensed.

Great, another car chase. It was only the second I'd been in, but one was more than enough. Last time, the car had flipped, and I'd been thrown across the outback. That was the same night I'd killed for the first time.

Pushing away the memory, I leaned forwards, looking in the passenger side mirror. The black SUV was still there, though a white van was separating us.

Ahead, the traffic lights flicked to amber, and the car roared forwards, chasing the red light. I looked over my shoulder and saw the van had slowed for the red, but the SUV swerved into the adjacent lane and picked up speed, flying across the intersection behind us.

Sliding back into my seat, I tightened the seatbelt and held on as Chaser slammed his foot on the gas.

The car roared forward, weaving sharply through traffic.

"I haven't got time for this shit," he muttered. "Hold on."

"Oh, I've already got a death grip going on here," I fired back.

We weaved through traffic, tires squealing as Chaser sharply turned the wheel. My stomach went left and right as the movement buffeted my body around, and Wren let out a terrified yelp from the backseat. Ahead, the traffic lights were red, but he didn't slow. My eyes widened as I saw cars and trucks crossing the intersection going the opposite way.

"Chaser..." I warned. "The light is red..."

"I know."

"What if—"

He must've pressed his foot on the accelerator all the way to the floor because I was pushed back into the seat as the car rocketed towards the busy crossroads.

"Chaser..." I said warily. "I don't like this..."

He ignored me and powered through the intersection, causing drivers to slam on their brakes. The sounds of crashing metal, breaking glass, and blasting horns reached my ears. I let out a yelp, holding on for dear life.

The car fishtailed slightly as Chaser weaved through the chaos, then we were clear.

"Don't do that again!" I screeched.

"Say that again when this is over."

Swallowing a pile of vomit, I looked over my shoulder, searching for the black SUV. It glinted behind us, following the path we'd forged through our self-made chaos back at the traffic light.

"They're still coming," Wren said, looking out the back, too. "We've got a bit of a lead on them, though."

"Good." Chaser turned the wheel, and we screeched into a side street before rocketing forwards. He turned again, this time down a narrow lane, then slammed his foot on the brake, shifted the car into reverse, and then planted his foot on the accelerator. I was flung forwards from the abrupt momentum, and I slammed my hands against the dash as we flew into another lane, then around into a random driveway before jerking to a stop.

"Smooth," I said

Wren twisted around in her seat. "Do you think we lost them?"

Chaser glanced out of the front window. "Don't know."

"You don't know?" I demanded. "So what...? We just sit here and wait for them to find us?"

Chaser grunted, unbuckled his seatbelt, and threw open the door.

"Where are you going?"

"Stay here and keep your heads down."

I did what he said and slid down in the seat. Flipping open the glove compartment, I pulled it out the gun and checked the barrel. There were still a couple of bullets left.

I glanced at Wren, who was looking a little pale. "Sorry to get you messed up in all this."

"It's okay," she murmured. "I kind of expected a few fireworks when you called."

"Still, I appreciate your help. I couldn't have managed it without you."

The witch smiled. "I guess."

Realising I'd won her trust, I grinned. I really liked her. If it wasn't for all the blood and explosions, we'd be the best of friends. We'd go shopping, out for coffee and cocktails, and do all the things normal friends did —a witch and a werewolf. How the tables had turned.

I lifted my head just enough so I could peer out of the back window and scanned for signs of Chaser. It wasn't long before he reappeared, jogging down the dilapidated lane.

"So?" I asked as we slid back into the driver's seat.

"We should be clear."

"Just like that? It was a little too easy if you ask me."

"We're fine, Sloane. I've been doing this a long time. I know when I've shaken a tail."

I looked at Wren, but she just shrugged. She was just along for the ride at this point.

Chaser gunned the engine, and we edged out of the driveway, down the lane, and back onto the street. He seemed satisfied we'd lost our tail, so we continued on our way again. He took us on a random path through

Melbourne's outer suburbs, but the black SUV didn't reappear.

Thankful for one thing going right today, I sank into my seat and wished as hard as I could for a bed... and at least five continuous minutes of not having someone try to kill us.

Chaser found us another nondescript motel on the fringes of society.

Eyeing the decaying building as we found our room, I was sure this was the place where dreams went to die and rot away. I wouldn't be surprised if half the clientele were sketchy. There was an upside, though— no one would ask any questions.

I opened the door and was immediately hit with the ripe scent of mothballs. Screwing up my nose, I walked inside and dumped my bag on the bed.

"You really know how to pick 'em," I drawled, wondering if Wren's room next door was any better.

"Believe me, I'd rather that hotel in the city," Chaser replied, closing the door.

"Honestly, I'd rather we sign up for the first manned space mission to colonise Mars."

"You need to sleep," he murmured, smoothing my hair behind my ear.

"Are you sure we lost them?"

He nodded, and my heart began to sink as I let

some of my guard down. Man, I was so tired, it was a wonder I hadn't collapsed yet, but sleep felt further away than it ever had. So many things were left unsaid.

"Chaser..."

He looked at me, his brow creasing. "What?"

"When..." I hesitated, and he raised his eyebrows. "What did King say to you?"

Chaser's whole stature changed in an instant. His shoulders tensed, his lip curled, and his eyes brimmed with a fury I'd never seen before.

I edged backwards, suddenly frightened of the man before me. I knew he had these feelings towards King, but seeing them on his face? It was something else entirely. He looked...manic. I decided I didn't like it.

I swallowed hard and centred myself. "Forget I asked."

Chaser was silent so long, I was starting to believe he'd spiralled into some kind of mental episode

"He's... There's a darkness in that man," he finally said. "He's terrifying, Sloane. He knew how to manipulate me into a position where I was nothing. Our whole plan, our whole existence, was a setup. It was predetermined long before I even laid eyes on you. We never had any chance."

"That's because he's a thousand-year-old vampire," I exclaimed, tugging on his sleeve. "This is what he breathes in and out. It's what he eats and shits. He's the king for a reason. All we have to do is..." I trailed off, knowing anything I could suggest would be lame as. I didn't know anything. My political science textbook couldn't help us now.

"What we have to do is give him what he wants," Chaser said. "Or run for the rest of our lives."

"What? No!" I curled my hand around his arm, my fingers biting into his flesh. "There's a third option here, Chaser. We have to turn his game around and screw him with it. We have to stand and *fight*."

"They know about the talisman by now. They know I'm alive. We won't be able to use it against them again. If we're caught, they'll rip it from my arm, and I'll be bound to King for eternity. Then they'll use me to get to you and you'll die in their ritual."

"Then we die knowing we tried."

"They will slaughter the pack, Sloane, and they'll kill Wren and Monroe. It's not just about us anymore."

I shook my head. "And you want to do nothing... knowing everyone will die?"

"Sloane... If we fail..." Chaser swallowed hard, his gaze lowering.

"We were going to do the same thing," I argued. "Nothing's changed."

"*Everything's* changed."

"No," I whispered, shaking my head. "You can't—"

A knock broke us apart, and I stared at the door, tensing up further. Chaser didn't hesitate, though. He strode across the room and peered through the peephole before opening the door and letting in a familiar hulking mass.

"Gasket!" I leapt across the room and flung myself into his arms, holding him tightly, inhaling his familiar scent of leather and motor oil. Gasket would talk sense into Chaser. I knew he would.

"Hey, kid," he said, his gravelly voice comforting as he returned my embrace. "I hear you've been on one hell of a ride."

"That's the understatement of the century."

"You came alone?" Chaser asked.

"Had to," Gasket replied. "Things are still up in the air."

"Why are you here?" I asked. "Isn't it a risk?"

Gasket nodded. "After Chaser told me what happened, I had to see you. Besides, things are getting dicey."

"Are you back at the compound?" I went on, firing off questions left, right, and centre. "The Hollow Men will look for us there first, and if they don't find us—"

"They haven't even twitched," the old wolf interrupted, cocking an eyebrow. "No sign of vampires in the northern suburbs. It's all quiet."

Not for long.

"Any word on the renegades?" Chaser butted in.

"They've blown away like a fart in the wind. We had a tail on them for a while, but they just disappeared. I don't like it, Chaser. Something's coming...something big. Wolves like those don't just disappear."

I frowned, not liking the lack of progress. We hadn't

made any either, so who was I to judge? The hole had just gotten bigger and darker.

"There isn't a mole in Fortitude, so I think one of the renegades called in a tip-off," he went on. "I dragged the pack across the coals, and none of them squawked. They won't, anyway. Not after what happened at the cottage." He glanced at me.

"Good," Chaser said. "That's the last thing we need."

"I don't think that matters," I declared.

"Huh?" Gasket glanced at me, clearly confused.

"The whole thing was a setup," I said before Chaser could butt in. "The Hollow Men—"

"*Sloane*," Chaser warned.

I didn't want to hear it. "Chaser was going to—"

"*Sloane*," Chaser barked. "The less Gasket knows, the better."

Gasket glanced between us, his brow creasing. Stroking his beard, he looked thoughtful for a moment. "I agree. I know you kids are in some trouble right now, but the less of a trail you can leave behind, the better. We're being attacked on two fronts, and Fortitude is strapped as it is keeping the renegades off you. The fact that we've lost their scent when they stink...that ain't good."

The more they talked, the more I felt like throwing something out the window. The men were making plans and the little girl had to pipe down. *Screw this.*

"Do whatever the hell you want," I snarled. "I'm

sick and tired of this shit."

"Sloane..."

"He offered himself up as a sacrifice," I said, pointing at Chaser. "His life for mine. That's not what I signed up for! This whole thing, this whole fight against King, is about both of us, and he wanted to hand himself over for me. He's going to do it again! I can see it in his eyes!"

Gasket glanced at Chaser. "That's love if I've ever seen it."

"I won't love a dead man!" I shouted.

Chaser flinched slightly. The movement was so fleeting, I almost missed it, but I'd hit him right where it hurt.

Gasket sighed, clearly out of his depth. This was something Chaser and I had to deal with.

"Whatever happens, I've got your back, kid," he murmured. "Okay?"

I knew he did, but right now, his words felt empty.

To Chaser, he said, "If that's what you want to do, you better think long and hard before you let anyone pull the trigger." He nodded towards the door. "Give me a minute alone with her, okay?"

Chaser scowled but honoured Gasket's request. He strode across the room and wrenched the door open. A moment later, it slammed behind him.

"He loves you," Gasket said. "He might not know how to show it, but he's trying to do whatever he can to keep you safe...and free."

"But I can't do it without him," I argued. "This whole thing is about *our* forever, not mine. I'm fighting this fight for him, Gasket."

"I know you are...but he's fighting it for you, too."

"I can't let him die," I whispered. "Not for me. He's already taken two bullets in the heart for me. I won't let him take a third."

Gasket's brow furrowed, and he grasped my shoulders. "Listen to me, kid. I know you've had a rough life. I know your daddy treated you like a thing. I know his actions got your mother murdered. I know you had to leave before you wound up the same way. But you're a grown woman now. You have to forget those things. The past ain't where your heart is at, girl. You're worth it, Sloane, you hear me? To me, to Fortitude, and especially to that cranky son of a bitch standing out there. I know you want the happily ever after, but sometimes sacrifice means—"

"I know," I interrupted. "I know."

"This fight is bigger than all of us," he murmured. "It might've started with you, but it's so much more. We're fighting for all our futures."

"It's just..." A tear spilled down my cheek, and I brushed it away with the back of my hand.

"You're in love with him," Gasket said, wiping away another tear. "I get it."

I nodded. "Hopelessly."

The old wolf smiled and shook his head. "Yeah. I know all about that."

CHAPTER 16

CHASER

Leaning against the side of the motel, I stared out across the car park to the bush beyond. Once you'd seen one hole, you'd seen them all.

The sun was roasting my shoulders, the black T-shirt I was wearing absorbing the heat. I wiped the sweat from my forehead with the back of my arm and pushed my sunglasses up.

Sloane and Gasket were talking in the room behind me, but I knew better than to listen at the door.

I won't love a dead man. Her admission meant more than she realised. I loved a dead woman for a century. I would always love Loretta in some way, but Sloane was here. She was *living,* flesh and blood.

The stress of this revenge plot was getting to everyone. The humid summer heat wasn't helping, either. I was constantly cold, my skin like ice, but the humidity still ate away at the edges of my patience like flesh-eating bacteria.

The door of the adjoining room opened and Wren appeared, her damp hair leaving a wet patch on the back of her singlet top.

When she saw me glowering, she ducked into the shade beside me. "Things not going well, huh?"

I raised an eyebrow.

"I don't have to have super hearing to hear the yelling," she added with a sigh.

"It's been one hell of a day."

"I'll say," she drawled.

We stood in silence for a moment until she worked up the courage to say, "I've been studying the spells around the ritual the Hollow Men plan to use on Sloane."

"The spells?" I asked, staring down at her. "How did you get them?"

"The Hollow Men forced my coven into working for them, remember?" Wren curled her lip and fiddled with the silver rings on her fingers. "I think they got it all wrong."

My anger faded some. "How?"

"I'm not sure yet, but nothing's changed regarding Sloane's involvement. They still need her blood for the ritual to work."

"Then why even bother telling me?" I drawled. My anger rose again, the fleeting spark of hope going straight out the proverbial window.

Wren bit her bottom lip, her cheeks flushing. Her brow creased as if she was choosing her words, then she snorted. "I have a way we can remove her from the equation. No Sloane, no ritual."

"Then why do you look like you're about to kill a puppy?" I sneered.

"Well, you're not entirely wring," she murmured. "I can suppress Sloane's werewolf side."

I looked the witch over, wondering how powerful she was. It sounded like the silver bullet we needed, but there was always a price with magic. They took from nature, and nature always found a balance... which almost always ended up biting someone in the arse.

"What's the catch?" I asked with a sigh.

"It'd be permanent."

"Have you told Sloane?"

"There wasn't time," Wren replied. "Besides, after everything that happened today, I don't think I can." She scuffed the toe of her shoe in the dirt. "I like her. I don't want to see her hurt."

I snorted. "And to think a week ago you were planning to sacrifice her to avenge your dead coven."

"I made a mistake," she hissed, turning to face me. "Like you've never done worse."

She had me there.

"If you take her werewolf side, you'd be erasing half her soul," I murmured. "The answer is no."

"She may not have a choice, Chaser."

I turned towards Wren, my emotions at a boiling point, but the door opened behind us before I could... I didn't know what I was going to do. Threaten her? *Probably*.

Gasket appeared, his boots crunching on loose gravel.

"Wren, there you are," the old wolf said. "I'm headed back to the city. You're welcome to come with me if you're sick of this grumpy bastard. You ride pillion before?"

Wren glanced at me, her eyes narrowed.

"Go," I snapped. "You've done enough here."

"There's more I can do at the compound anyway," she said, not bothering to hide her dislike of me. "You know where I am if you change your mind."

Gasket sighed and nodded towards his motorcycle. "Give me a minute with Chaser and then we'll head out."

The witch nodded and scurried back inside her room, slamming the door closed behind her.

"You're a real people-person, you know that?" the wolf said with a grunt. "You need to work on your approachability."

I knew I was an abrasive piece of work. I owed Wren an apology, especially after she'd risked her life to save mine, but I had no doubt that she'd done it for Sloane, not me.

"Sloane calmed down yet?" I asked, pushing off the wall.

"She almost lost you today... How do you think she is?"

"Do I want to go back in there?"

"Don't be too hard on her," Gasket replied. "I know you're in a bad spot—"

"Bad spot? That's what you call it?" I snorted and looked away. I couldn't deal with his fatherly nonsense today.

"If you think getting yourself killed without even fighting is the answer, then you're more messed-up than I ever believed possible."

"Careful, old man," I drawled.

"I've got to get back." He fished his keys out of his pocket and spun them around his finger.

"And?" I prodded.

"I'll do what I can to track the renegades. They won't get away, not after what they've done to harm her, Chaser. If we have to kill every last one of them, then that's what we'll do. No mercy."

"Good. I've got enough names on my list already."

"Chaser... This war isn't just about you," he said. "I told her that, too. It's bigger than just you and her settling scores."

I glared at him, not trusting myself to speak.

"The pack doesn't turn it's back on family." He clapped me on the shoulder and grinned. "*Brother*."

"Bloody hell," I drawled, rolling my eyes.

"Just pull yourself together, eh?" He nodded towards the motel room. "Remember what you're fighting for, Chaser. Remember it, and don't forget again."

"Or what?"

"You don't want to know."

Wren appeared again, not even looking at me as she approached Gasket's motorcycle. He handed her his open-faced helmet and as she fussed with the chin strap, I grabbed her arm.

My touch made the witch flinch, and she glared up at me. "What?"

"I'm..." I grimaced. "I'm sorry."

Her expression softened a minuscule amount, but it was all the apology I could wring out of my hardened heart.

"I'll be in touch," Gasket said as my hand fell away.

He flung his leg over his motorcycle and waited as Wren climbed on the back. Turning the key in the ignition, the beast roared into life. He threw me one last look, then they tore out of the lot and onto the road.

I waited, listening to the sound of the motorcycle fade into the distance, thinking about what the old wolf had just said.

Remember what you're fighting for.

Love. I supposed that was what he was hinting at. Love, family, and a future without fear.

Love. Whatever that was.

I turned back to the motel room and grasped the door handle. Love, family, and a future. I'd been alone for so long, lost in misery. When had all those things found their way to me?

I didn't know, but Gasket was right. I'd forgotten what I was fighting for.

Finally, I opened the door.

CHAPTER 17

SLOANE

*H*opelessly.

The word held so many conflicting definitions, I wasn't sure which one to focus on.

Outside, I heard Gasket's motorcycle start, and I looked towards the door, knowing the two men would've had words. I just wanted... What did I want?

Chaser's end echoed Marini's, but where my father didn't care about my mother's murder, Chaser cared too much about the murder of Loretta. Just us being here, working against King and the Hollow Men, was evidence of that. After all we'd been through, I still harboured jealousy over a dead woman.

He was right about one thing. I'd locked everything away rather than deal with it. Indifference wasn't a badge of honour; it was the mark of death.

It was ironic in a way. I was becoming the cold, unfeeling one, and Chaser was warming up. Who would we be at the end of all this? If we survived, would our relationship?

I turned my mum's engagement ring over in my palm and studied the light refracting through the diamond. At least, I thought it was a diamond. It could be a cubic zirconia or a slice of glass for all I knew. It didn't matter. It was the only thing I had of hers, even though my father had given it to her.

The motel room door opened, letting in a shaft of sunlight and Chaser. Murky orange light enveloped the space once more as he shut out the world.

"Wren went back to the city with Gasket."

I didn't look up. "Oh…"

"What's that?" he asked, sitting beside me.

"My mum's engagement ring." I held up my palm so he could see the gold band.

"Where'd you find that?"

"I stole it from Marini's room the night of the coup." I sighed. "I went after him then, but he wasn't there. I know you didn't want me to be part of all that, but…"

"I was trying to protect you," he murmured.

"I know, but I needed to fight my own battles."

"Is that why you went after him at DeLuca's cottage?"

An unexpected wave of emotion clouded my mind, and I waited a moment for it to clear.

"I know I said I was going to kill him," I said. "I believed I would, but when it came down to it, I wasn't so sure I could go through with it. But I knew he wouldn't change his mind about sacrificing me, and I knew I couldn't pull the trigger. So, I let the wolf take over." I lowered my gaze. "All that other stuff, the revenge, the hatred...those reasons came after. But..."

"But?"

I glanced at him before turning towards the window. "I liked it." I looked at him again, trying to gauge his response, but his face was as stoic as ever. "I don't want to feel like that again. It brought out the parts of me that echo Marini. I don't want to be him. It was like a sick addiction was trying to drag me away, and I...I didn't want to admit it. All I want is to let the wolf take over and tear everything apart. To feel the blood of my enemies in my mouth—" I choked and covered my face with my hands. "*Oh, God.*"

He didn't say anything, and my mind began filling in the blanks with depressing action items. I'd become the thing he hated. He didn't want to love me if I was like Marini. He'd realised he'd made a mistake. He'd signed himself up to a death sentence he no longer believed in.

I began to panic, the tragedy of my life flashing before my eyes. "I know you said you'd die for me, but saying the words... If you can't say it, do you really believe those things?"

Chaser's expression closed so fast, it was like he'd slammed a door in my face.

Oh God, I've screwed everything up. I've pushed too

hard, and now he's realised he wants out.

"If this ends up being one-sided, if it's just the danger and adrenaline that's made you feel this way, then I don't care," I declared, rising to my feet. "I'd rather have loved on my own than not at all." *Shit, talk about self-torture.* "I can't let you sacrifice yourself again..." A sick realisation hit me square in the heart. He wasn't doing this for me. "You're not... You're doing this for—"

I turned my back on him, humiliation heating my cheeks. Where did I get off thinking I was so special? I was just a wolf who could change at will, not some supernatural goddess who was owed worship. I was a freak of nature, that was all.

"I don't know what I expected," I muttered. "A happy ending? In this life? *Yeah, right.*"

I thought I was okay with Chaser's quest to avenge Loretta. She was dead, and I was alive. Maybe I was just a full-blown head case.

"If I don't belong here, then where do I belong?" I stared at him, my throat aching. "Gasket said I was worth it, but I can't see it. All I've done since I walked into your life is screw it up. You've been shot and captured, lost everything, lost your place at Fortitude, *died twice*, and now you... Your revenge is for her, and I'm just... I'm just a way to get there."

Chaser was like a statue, sitting on the end of the bed staring at me. Whatever he thought about my self-destruction, he didn't comment. He didn't even blink.

"Answer me," I exclaimed. I was ranting like a fool and destroying the last shred of hope I had in my life.

Everyone wants to be loved, I thought. *But what if I'm meant to love alone? Can I live, knowing I'm destined to self-destruct? Maybe I should just let King sacrifice me. It'd save them all, wouldn't it?*

"*Say something!*" I screeched.

"I love you."

It was my turn to stare. I blinked, my hands trembling.

Chaser rose to his feet and stood before me, his hands cupping my face. His touch burned my skin, his eyes staring deep into mine.

"I hear you," he murmured. "We're going to be okay."

"But—"

"We just have to do one more thing before forever, remember?"

A tear slipped from my eye, dripping down my cheek like a little traitor. I didn't cry. I *never* cried.

"I'm not going to die, Sloane. I won't let him touch you."

"The ritual," I began, my voice wavering.

"Screw the ritual."

My breath caught.

"We both get out of this, no matter what," he added, resting his forehead against mine. "It's non-negotiable. We'll find another way."

"Chaser, I..."

"We lost our way for a while, but we're back. Okay?"

I froze, the tenderness in his expression haunting. When his lips took mine, I melted into his touch, unable to do anything but wrap myself around his being. I worked up the nerve to say those words again, my soul trembling with excitement, but before I could get them out, Chaser pushed me back onto the bed.

I gasped in surprise as he covered my body with his, the weight of him igniting a spark inside me.

"Chaser..."

We wrapped around one another, caught up in the heat of the moment. His words echoed in my heart, my outburst seeming foolish now that we were here.

We were all there was. Our enemies were nothing. Our revenge was nothing. *Our fear was nothing.*

"This," he said with a heavy breath, "this is what I want... I want to be with you. I don't care what you are. I don't care about your blood. I just want to be with *you.*"

He didn't have to say any more than that. I understood. There were no more barriers between us —no more doubts, no more secrets, and no more fear. We were *together*. The same.

I ran my hands along the curve of his back, relishing the strength coiled in his muscles. Lingering on one of his many scars, I moved and his lips found mine.

CHAPTER 18

CHASER

As Sloane and I lay together after we'd worn ourselves out, my arm circled her slender form. She'd gotten thinner. All this stress had been taking its toll.

Nestled along my side with her cheek on my chest, Sloane's fingers traced an old scar on my ribs. Draped was an appropriate word. Sloane was draped over me. She draped like no other woman had.

"Where did we go wrong?" she murmured, her cheek moving against my chest as she spoke. "I've been trying to pinpoint it, but I can't."

"Don't dwell," I replied. "Dwelling won't change anything."

"Are we safe here?"

"I don't know."

I glanced at the bedside table. Her mother's ring glinted in the artificial light filtering through the crack in the curtains. She'd been holding it a lot—studying the diamond, learning the curves of the gold claws holding the stone in place—but she never put it on. I assumed she was thinking about her, but she never voiced her thoughts.

"Do you want to talk about your mother?" I asked.

"Why?"

"Her ring..."

"No," she said after a moment. "I don't want to talk about that."

I pulled in a deep breath, my chest rising, then let it out. It wasn't a sigh, it was a reset. A deep breath to fill my lungs with life.

"Chaser?"

"Yeah?"

Headlights lit up the window, and I tensed, but the car beyond kept going. Whoever it was, wasn't here for us.

"Are we just going to wait?" she asked.

"Yes."

"Then?"

"I don't know," I admitted.

"We'll figure something out. I'll cut my hair, bleach it blonde. Get facial reconstruction surgery."

"That's a bit extreme." I snorted and dragged my fingers through her hair. "Ten days."

"That's a bit specific," she said, twisting my words into a comeback. "Why ten?"

"I've been thinking..."

"You can think?" Her head rose, and her eyes sparkled in the half-light. "*The horror.*"

"Some men can multitask," I retorted, my lips twisting into a smile.

Sloane propped herself up on her elbow and placed her fingers on my mouth. "I like when you do that."

I narrowed my eyes. "Smile?"

"You brood a lot."

"I thought brooding was sexy."

She laughed and shook her head, her hair falling forwards and spilling onto my bare chest. The fact she could laugh with King's threats hanging over her head was unbelievable. It just proved her strength even more. Her insecurities didn't weaken her one bit—they just showed how human she was underneath all that werewolf.

I was still raw after my admission, but there was a seed of fear that was growing along with it. Caring let in emotions I'd tried to forget a long time ago. The anguish of loss was something I might struggle with for the rest of my life, but Sloane...she understood.

That's why I knew I had to tell her about Wren's spell. I couldn't keep a secret like that from her, not after all she'd suffered. Sloane deserved the truth.

"Wren told me about a spell," I murmured.

"What kind of spell?"

"One that will suppress your werewolf side."

She perked up, her eyes widening. "And it would

make my blood useless to King? The ritual wouldn't work?"

I nodded. "But..."

Sloane sighed sharply, her breath fluttering against my chest. "There's always a *but*."

"It would be permanent."

"I'd have to give up the wolf inside me?"

I nodded. "I told her no. Not under any circumstances."

She let out a cry of frustration and pushed away from me, rising. "You have no right to make that choice for me!"

"Sloane." I sat up and grasped her wrists, pulling her back towards me. "It's not a simple matter. Suppressing your werewolf side would be like cutting out half your soul. You were born to be a wolf. *It's who you are.*"

"But if it can save everyone—"

"No," I interrupted. "Do you really believe King would just give up if he didn't have you? That there wouldn't be any repercussions?"

"No." She pulled in a shaking breath, her eyes widening. "He'd still kill everyone."

I nodded and wrapped my arms around her. "I won't let you carve out your soul, Sloane."

"Freedom, love, forever," she whispered, her eyes shining in the darkness.

I sat on the edge of the bath, watching Sloane dry herself with one of the threadbare motel towels.

Another day had passed in blissful solitude. It seemed our whereabouts were still a secret, but the comings and goings at the motel still had me on edge.

The downtime had forced me to think more than ever. The more I dwelled on my failed attempt to get into the *Halcyon*, the more I realised I'd been impatient. I was caught up in the chase and never thought about all the consequences. I hadn't thought like King. *Embody your enemies, and you can find their weaknesses*. I'd focused on the wrong things.

The rim of the bath dug into my arse, and I shifted before settling back down. Those were strange words. Settling down. Sloane had said something about horses and green things a while back.

"When this is over, what do you want to do?" I asked. "Do you really want to go to Tasmania?"

She stopped squeezing the moisture out of her hair and looked at me. "You remember that?"

"Of course, I do."

"I don't know. What do you want?"

I hesitated, frowning at her question. It was simple enough, but I hadn't thought farther than the moment of revenge. Sloane was what I wanted, but anything more specific than that and I was at a loss. I couldn't go back to my old life, and even though Gasket would likely welcome me back into the ranks of Fortitude, I wasn't sure going back to the compound was the right place for me. I was a vampire, and vampires didn't belong in werewolf packs.

Sloane, though...she was alpha. It didn't matter if she'd put Gasket in charge, it was she who killed Marini. Wolf law wasn't just a bunch of words someone wrote down, it was supernatural. It was law bound by blood and magic. Sloane was the Fortitude alpha.

"Love, family, and a future," I said.

"Huh?"

"It's something Gasket reminded me of."

"Is that what he was beating into your head out there?" She smirked, combing her fingers through her hair.

"I closed myself off for so long, I didn't realise what I was doing," I said as she wrapped the towel around her body. "I wasn't giving you a choice."

"Oh, Chaser..." She sat beside me and leaned her head on my shoulder. "I found a way to make them, anyway."

I snorted and rubbed my palm on her thigh.

"And if it comes down to it, I'll be the one to decide about Wren's spell. Okay?"

I tensed, not liking that she would have to even consider it, but I nodded my agreement.

"So, we've had time to rest and figure things out," she went on. "What now? I know you've been thinking about it. Care to elaborate on your mysterious 'ten days'?"

I breathed deeply, savouring her scent.

Sloane was a mortal wolf, Marini was, too...and so was King. He wasn't an immortal tyrant, not like the founding vampires—the first of our kind—who could only be killed by one specific twist of nature. He might have a legion of vampires and witches surrounding him, but he was still vulnerable. There had to be a chink in his armour, an angle he hadn't thought of.

Everything could be killed because nature always found a way. It was magic 101, even I knew that.

And I would find the way.

"War," I replied, leaning my forehead against hers. "An all-out war."

CHAPTER 19

SLOANE

I peered out the window at the motel beyond, the eerie light of predawn making the bush look ghostly.

"What are we doing exactly?" I asked when I heard Chaser rustle around in our bag.

He was double- and triple-checking we had everything we needed. He'd whittled down our belongings back in Melbourne, then I'd whittle some more, so there wasn't much to pack, but I couldn't fault him for being obsessive.

He still hadn't explained his ten-day super plan. It was a specific timeline, and 'all-out war' wasn't exactly the step-by-step I was hoping for.

Honestly, I was at a loss. I had no idea what to do next.

"First, we've got to leave," Chaser said. "We can't stay in the same place for more than a day or two."

I hoped he knew where we were going because I was lost. There were still stars in the sky, it was that early. I shivered and let the curtains fall back into place.

"The bush confuses me," I said.

"Why's that?"

"It's freezing out, but once the sun comes up, we'll be having a BBQ on the hood of the car."

"Sunny-side up?" Chaser cocked an eyebrow.

"Hilarious. I like scrambled."

I slid my arms into my denim jacket and flipped up the collar, even though I'd be boiling by the time the sun fully rose. Next, I reached for my revolver and slipped it into the inside pocket. It was the perfect coat for stashing things. I disliked carrying a handbag, so pockets were a dream come true. The butt hung out, the mother-of-pearl shimmering in the light, but it stayed put. Once I buttoned up the front, it'd be secure. Something told me having access to a quick draw was a good idea.

"Ready?" Chaser asked, throwing the bag over his shoulder.

I nodded. I was ready, as in packed and dressed, but mentally...? I was getting there. *Slowly*.

Chaser opened the door and stepped outside with me right behind him, and when we realised we weren't alone, my heart twisted.

A group of werewolves were lined up in the lot outside, their motorcycles behind them. The motel grounds were narrow out here, and the line of shrubs and gnarled trees bordering the edge of the property narrowed the space significantly. They must've wheeled their bikes into the lot because we never heard any engines. We hadn't heard a single squeak, and now we were hemmed in with no way to escape.

Chaser grasped my arm, and we came to a stop. Six guns were pointed right at us—pistols, revolvers, and one shotgun. My reflexes kicked in, and I slid my revolver from my inside pocket.

I narrowed my eyes and took in each face, memorising them all. I recognised most of them from Fortitude—the dregs of society. When I got to their leader, I felt like throwing up in my mouth.

"Rocket."

"Sloane," he replied. "You've got a lot to answer for, young lady." His mouth curved into a grin as he shook his gun at me.

One thing I noticed about them, they were well rested, their motorcycles shone despite the thin layer of dust from their ride from the city, and their jackets and vests had new emblems on them. A flaming skull with the words, Hollow Riders MC, Melbourne. They'd styled themselves after a bloody motorcycle gang.

"I left you for dead," Chaser said. "You should be rotting in the ground."

"Hoo boy!" Rocket exclaimed. "I bested cold, old Chaser. I never thought I'd see the day. I'll have to give my regards to Gasket. He led us here, the stupid old dog, then he took your witch!"

I curled my lip, resisting the urge to kick him in the balls.

"Chaser..." I tugged at his arm, ignoring Rocket's goading. "Their jackets..."

"Let me introduce you to the new lieutenants of the Hollow Riders Motorcycle Club, the newest East Coast werewolf pack." Rocket smirked and spread his arms wide. "King sends his regards."

"You're with them," I murmured. "You're on the Hollow Men's payroll." That was why Gasket lost their scent.

They had a new master.

"Bingo, sweetheart. Where there's an opportunity for profitable mayhem, we're goin' to take it. Fortitude was going down, with or without you ripping apart your daddy. You just gave us the opportunity to spread our wings."

"Some wings," Chaser muttered.

"King wants you alive." Rocket hocked, then spat on the asphalt. "You know what that means." He straightened up and aimed his gun at Chaser, and the other wolves followed suit. "On your knees."

My fingers itched to curl around some mother-of-pearl. There was no way in hell Rocket and his gang of rejects were going to best us. Not after everything we'd struggled through to get here. I glanced at Chaser, and he nodded.

"Be quick," he murmured, letting me know he was on the same wavelength. "I'll follow your lead."

Reaching behind me, I wrapped my fingers around the revolver and pulled it out. I fired, making the wolves scatter, and dove behind our car. Chaser was beside me, his gun in his hands, the safety off. I was never more thankful to have enhanced speed.

"Bitch!" Rocket roared.

"Eat shit, arsehole!" I screeched as gunfire rained down on us. Thankfully, the car took most of the brunt, though the motel behind us had a few new holes in the wall.

"We can't take them all," Chaser said.

"I can turn," I told him.

"They'd shoot you before—"

"*I can do it.*"

"No." He grabbed my arm. "This isn't a fight we can win. There's twelve of them and two of us. I don't care how strong you are."

The trigger clicked on my revolver, and I cursed. I reloaded, spun the barrel back into place, waited for a break in gunfire, then poked my head back up. Firing, I used my last six shots as best I could. I aimed for Rocket, but he ducked behind another guest's car and the bullet sailed right past. I tried again and again; I felt like I was playing a sick game of whack-a-mole.

I pulled the trigger, and nothing happened. Cursing, I knelt back behind the car.

"I'm out," I said to Chaser. "Got any bright ideas?"

"We've got to get away from here," he replied.

"Where do we go? We don't have a plan."

Another wave of gunfire pinned us behind the car. A shotgun pellet shattered the window above our heads, and I shielded my face, flinching as granulated glass fell down the back of my jacket.

"Fortitude," Chaser said, shoving the last clip into his gun as sirens wailed in the distance.

"The city? King will expect us to go there!"

The sirens were getting louder as yet another problem approached.

"We have no other choice," he hissed. "We'll be protected there."

"How?" I covered my head with my arms as another rain of bullets smacked into the car. "They shot out our fuel tank."

Chaser pointed to the row of motorcycles. "Do you know how to ride?"

My eyes widened, and I nodded. I'd learned during a rebellious phase as a teenager, then I'd had a refresher when I started my apprenticeship at the Fortitude garage. I hadn't gone farther than around the neighbourhood back then, so cruising the highway at full tilt had my blood running.

"*Sloane, the sirens.*"

I grimaced. "It won't matter if there are no keys in the ignition."

"They're cocky," he said. "They didn't expect a firefight. There'll be keys."

Chaser was right. We had to make a break for it before the cops arrived.

The gunfire subsided when the renegades realised we weren't fighting back.

"It's over!" Rocket shouted. "Come out, and we'll make this easy on you. King wants you both alive, but he said nothin' about the condition."

Chaser looked at me. "I'll cover you."

"What about you?" I whispered.

"I've been in worse positions," he replied. "I'll be right behind you."

Nodding, I stashed the revolver in my inside pocket. It was useless without bullets, but I didn't want to leave it behind.

Knowing Chaser only had one clip in his gun, I waited for his cue. There was no margin for error in this. It was either flee or die. *Don't look back.*

"Go!"

I sprang to my feet, pushing off the ground with all the strength I could muster. Sprinting across the lot, the deafening bang of gunfire covered my escape. Throwing my leg over the closest motorcycle, a Harley Sportster, my hands trembled as I fumbled with the controls. Thankfully, Chaser was right about the renegades being arrogant—the keys were still in the damn thing.

A surge of adrenaline drove me onwards, and I yanked out the choke and turned the key, wishing it was easier to start one of these hulking beasts. Pulling the clutch on, I shifted the gear into neutral and pressed the start button. Gunfire popped behind me, and I lowered my head as the bike roared into life. I didn't have time to wait for the engine to warm up, so I shifted into first and hit the accelerator. Gasket would have a fit, knowing I was riding a Harley with the choke on, but considering the circumstances, I didn't have a choice.

I almost lost my balance as I sped across the motel lot, the bike wobbling underneath me. I heard another engine start, followed by angry shouts, and hoped it was Chaser.

"After them!" I heard Rocket shout, but his voice was snatched away by the wind as I tore out onto the highway.

Glancing over my shoulder, the Harley wobbled slightly, and I sighed in relief when I saw Chaser gaining on me, and a row of flashing lights farther behind. The motel faded into the distance, but the glint of the remaining motorcycles followed us out onto the road.

Chaser came up alongside me, looking smooth as, the sound of the engines mingling.

"You okay?" he shouted over the road noise.

"Fine!"

"Can you handle the bike?"

"Piece of cake!"

He glanced over his shoulder. "They're gaining."

Bushland stretched on either side of the highway,

the rugged trees too dense for us to pull off. To the left were the beginnings of a rocky range of low mountains —the Macedon Ranges. We could lose them there.

I gestured to the road before us. "Lead the way."

Chaser nodded and moved ahead. A kilometre down the highway, he turned off onto a smaller road, and we weaved through the rocky landscape, the twists and turns hiding us from what was behind and in front.

Chaser slowed and drifted to the side after a few kilometres, the wheels of his bike hitting gravel. I followed his lead, and we edged into the rugged landscape, using the rocks and ancient gum trees to hide us from the road.

Chaser cut his engine, and I did the same, the silence of the wild feeling more deafening than the roar of two Harleys. Throwing his leg over, he strode across the grass, then began climbing up the side of a boulder, finding handholds in the uneven rock.

I stashed our bag in a cleft between two jagged boulders, *just in case*, and climbed up beside Chaser. The whole region was dotted with the prehistoric remains of ancient volcanoes and lava tubes, the scattered boulders all that remained of the chaotic, fiery past. Today, it sheltered us from the Hollow Riders and the cops...who I hoped had slowed down the former.

"Anything?" I asked.

"Not so far."

I breathed deeply, catching a metallic scent in the air. I looked at Chaser, realising he'd been bleeding. Grabbing his arm, I pulled him around. "You've been shot."

He shrugged me off. "It's just a scratch." He rolled up the hem of his T-shirt, showing me his side. "It's already healed."

I ran my fingers across his skin, but he was right. There was a smear of blood, but whatever wound had torn open his flesh was gone. Honestly, it was a miracle it wasn't worse.

When I was satisfied he was fine, we sat among the rocks, watching the road and listening for sounds of pursuit. It wasn't long before the telltale rumble of a convoy echoed across the rugged landscape. The sun rose behind us, colouring the rolling green and grey hills with sharp light, the heat already turning up several notches. If it wasn't for the ominous buzz of our enemies, it'd be beautiful.

I tensed as a glint of silver flashed in the distance, moving along the road we'd just been on.

"They could see our tire tracks," I whispered, terrified my voice would carry even though they wouldn't be able to hear us over their engines.

"I don't think they're smart enough to track out here," Chaser replied. "Those men have spent their lives in the city."

"They could sniff us out," I said.

"I know these wolves. They'll drive right past."

"Then they'll go straight to the compound."

"Where Wren and Gasket have been working to fortify the place against them and the Hollow Men." Chaser placed a reassuring hand on my shoulder. "We're going to get out of this, Sloane. They won't find us."

I sighed. "If you say so..."

Nestled among the expanse, we watched as ten motorcycles—and twelve men—rolled past. The Hollow Riders never had a chance in hell spotting us.

The cops, however, were nowhere to be seen, and not even the echo of a stray siren reached our supernatural ears.

We waited an hour before descending, then climbed on the motorcycles and returned to the road. Doubling back, we found our way to the main route and turned towards Melbourne, the only road open to us now.

CHAPTER 20

SLOANE

Chaser and I rode across the gentle roll of farmland northwest of the city, following the highway towards Melbourne. Drought had turned the grass a yellowish-brown and even the eucalyptus trees seemed washed out, but the ride was smooth enough, the wind buffering the heat cast by the harsh rays of the sun.

We stopped for petrol at a little town off the highway and called Gasket to let him know we were incoming. My gaze was constantly over my shoulder, but nothing appeared—nothing ominous, anyway. We kept our heads down, stuck to the speed limit, and did our best to be inconspicuous as two Harley Davidson motorcycles would allow. It seemed we were in the clear...for now.

It was late afternoon by the time we rolled into the Fortitude compound. Gasket was waiting for us in the garage, and the roller door rose as we turned into the driveway. Driving into the safety of the shop, our engines fell into silence as he closed us inside.

Jumping off my bike, I smacked my arse, trying to get the feeling back into both cheeks. Finally, I patted my windblown cheeks and hoped someone had left some moisturiser behind, because something told me a bunch of burly werewolves weren't that interested in skin care.

"I led them right to you," Gasket grumbled. "If I'd known, I would never have come out there."

"You couldn't have known," Chaser replied, shucking off our duffel bag. "You didn't know. We got out, so there's no use getting angry about it."

"Bested by Rocket." Gasket scratched his beard, looking sheepish. "I never thought I'd see the day."

I rolled my shoulders. "This whole thing has been one mess up after the next." Gasket opened his mouth, and I held up a hand. "Nuh-uh, don't even say it. Believe me, *I know*."

"I was going to say nice motorcycle, kid."

"*Nice save.*" I dusted off my hands. "Where's Wren? She doing okay?"

"Yeah," Gasket replied. "She's been weaving her magic wand and pouring over that crazy book of hers. I think she wants to talk to you when you've settled."

My curiosity peaked and I nodded. "Sure. Okay."

"Let's talk about this later," Chaser said. "We've got to clean up."

My stomach growled, breaking the rising anger in the garage, and I slapped a hand over my gut.

"You want something to eat, kid?" Gasket asked, glancing at Chaser. "We've got a new cook."

Chaser's expression contorted into annoyance, and he walked towards the compound.

"Where are you going?" the old wolf called out.

"I owe Monroe a punch in the face," Chaser replied, not breaking stride.

Gasket raised his eyebrows, looking at me expectantly.

"He gave us useless information in exchange for all this," I explained. "A black eye is the least of that guy's worries."

"Well, he better not hit him too hard because that wrinkly vampire cooks a mean steak."

"Is that all you can think of?" I retorted as we followed Chaser inside.

Gasket took the duffel bag and threw it over his shoulder. "As I see it, Monroe is a washed-up old man, whose life was one step away from a stake through the heart. Can't blame him for wanting to cash in rather than end up a wrinkled prune. Maybe he really did believe his information was good, or maybe he played Chaser from the beginning. Either way, he's going to fit right in around here."

The compound was empty as we made our way to the kitchens. With half the pack gone and the women and kids off in Wagga Wagga, it was deathly quiet. Not the greatest choice of words, but the closer we go to our destination, the noisier it became.

"I swear, I thought it was good!" an unknown voice shouted.

I glanced at Gasket as we stepped into the kitchen, but the old wolf was grinning at the scene before us.

Chaser had a pudgy African-American man up against the wall, his hands fisted into a greasy apron. I assumed this was the mysterious Monroe. I sniffed the air and let out a *humph*. Something was cooking, and it smelled really good.

"Nothing like a little tussle to grease the wheels," Gasket said in amusement.

"I don't appreciate being played," Chaser snarled. "Especially when the life of the woman I love is at stake."

Gasket threw me a look. "He said that?"

"It's a Christmas miracle," I replied. "You really going to let him punch the guy?"

Gasket shrugged. "Men like to work things out with their fists. Besides, it ain't like the guy can't take it. He'll heal just fine."

I rolled my eyes and strode forwards. I'd seen enough violence to last me a lifetime, with a great deal of it happening this morning. Monroe looked as threatening as a kitten in a basket of cotton buds.

"Chaser," I said, standing beside the two men. "Let him go."

Chaser's lip curled.

"Don't be a bully," I said with a pout. "Because if this guy screws with us again, I'll blow his head off with a shotgun." I directed my gaze to Monroe, who began shaking like a leaf. "I'm Sloane, by the way. *The woman he loves.*"

Behind us, Gasket started to laugh, the sound echoing around the kitchen. "She'll do it, you know."

I slapped my hand on Chaser's shoulder. "The guy's been sufficiently scared to hell and back. You can let him go now."

He glanced at me and let Monroe go, taking a few steps back.

We stood there in silence for a moment until things began to get a little awkward. The guy sure knew how to keep his mouth shut, which was a good start. The second item on the action list was food.

"So…" I craned my neck to see what was in the pot on the stove, "what's cooking?"

I opened the door to my bedroom and breathed in the unfamiliar scent. Why was it that after so long away, a place that'd become familiar felt so alien when you went back to it?

Stepping inside, I guessed I was just thankful for a place to rest that didn't include looking over my shoulder. It'd been a long time since I felt completely safe somewhere. It was the ultimate irony that it happened to be at the Fortitude compound.

"I never thought I'd be back here," I said, looking around. "At least, not this soon."

"We know this place," Chaser said, sliding his hand over the small of my back. "We can defend it if we need to."

"Hopefully, it won't come to that." I turned and curled my fingers into his shirt. "We better take the fight to them."

"King will be expecting it."

"I know, but we can't wait for them to come looking. We won't win that parade." All the Hollow Men's resources, paired with the Hollow Riders, against forty werewolves, me, Chaser, Monroe, and Wren? Yeah, no chance.

"So," I went on. "What was that ten-days thing? You never got a chance to tell me about it. I'm still curious."

Chaser shrugged. "It was the plan I was going to follow the first time. Before they..." He coughed and made a face. "I knew things were getting dicey, so I made provisions."

"You can talk about her, you know," I said. "All that stuff I said..." I felt my cheeks heat, and I lowered my head. "That was just my insecurities talking. I mean, I've never had this before. I was afraid it would never be like—"

"*Shh*," he murmured. "We worked that out."

"Hell, I'm just embarrassed."

"Don't be."

I looked up at him and smiled. "When did you get so soft?"

He made a face and tugged me close. "Don't say that word out loud."

"Soft," I declared. "Soft, soft, *soft*." Turning, I set the bag on the end of my bed and dusted off the front of my T-shirt.

"You're very happy," Chaser declared. "After this morning, I was expecting to have a fight on my hands."

"Ironically, I feel safe here, despite the memories."

"The air is different." He glanced around, taking in the room.

"Maybe staying here wouldn't be such a bad idea," I murmured.

"What about Tasmania?"

I shrugged. "When I think about the people here, the ones left behind..." I sighed and thought about Gasket. He'd been the father I'd never had, though we hadn't been close in years—not until I'd come back with Chaser. Gasket had become the fun uncle, making sure I was kept away from the influence of the pack, had food in my belly, and was safe from Marini's violence. When I'd been shipped off to foster care, I realised he'd been more of a dad to me than my biological one. He'd been trying to save me from all this, but life had a way of catching up.

"Wherever you want to go, I'll follow," Chaser

murmured. "Tasmania, Darwin, even to bloody Siberia if you want."

"There's no way in hell I'm going to Siberia. I hate the constant heat, but that's a little extreme, don't you think?"

"I was going for remoteness."

"A shack in the bush would've been remote enough." I began to have visions of rugged mountain men and a lumberjack Chaser throwing me over his shoulder. *That wouldn't be so bad...*

He grinned and sat on the bed, patting the mattress beside him. "Let me tell you about my plan. It'll have to be revised now that the Hollow Riders are a thing."

I sat next to him, my leg pressing against his, and relished his warmth. I stared at our boots, both laces stained with red dust and nodded.

"Let's go out with a bang, huh?"

Chaser grinned and knocked his boot into mine. "I was planning on it."

CHAPTER 21

SLOANE

I woke the next morning to an empty bed.

Rolling over, I smiled as I saw a hastily scrawled note from Chaser on the bedside table. *Talking with Gasket*. He really did have horrible handwriting.

After a hot shower, I found my way to the garage in search of the two most important men in my life. Glancing around the dark space, I couldn't spy them, but I found another crew instead.

"Sloane!"

I grinned as Ratchet waved me over. A whole bunch of familiar faces had gathered around the motorcycles that Chaser and I had stolen from the Hollow Riders. It still felt weird calling them that, kind of pathetic, actually. I bit my lip to stop myself from laughing—it really wasn't something to joke about—and went to stand with the guys.

"Hey," I said, punching Spike on the arm. "Long time."

"Couple of weeks," he replied. "You good?"

"It depends on your definition of good." I made a face and glanced around at the others.

Stewie, Hopper, Ratchet, Spike, and Watts each had a beer in their hands and seemed happy enough to see me despite all the shit I'd gotten them into.

"How's Rhodes?" I asked, remembering he got shot at the cottage. That night and everything before it seemed as if it were covered in a haze—as if it had happened to someone else. I wondered why that was.

"Butcher patched him up," Hopper said. "He's in Wagga Wagga with DeLuca lookin' after the girls."

"Don't let Shondra hear you refer to her as a girl," Spike said with a chuckle.

"She's my woman," the wolf immediately shot back and flipped the younger man the bird.

I frowned, knowing the guys missed their other halves. I hoped whatever Chaser and Gasket were discussing would help bring a swift end to this. If I were separated from Chaser... Well, hell had nothing on it.

"Wanna beer, Sloane?" Ratchet asked.

"It's a bit early for that," I replied, raising my eyebrows.

"Dark days call for partyin' when we can," Watts quipped.

I tensed and looked at the two motorcycles. "Anything we can do with these? Scratch off the serial numbers? Strip them down?"

"You want to strip down a Harley Davidson?" Spike's mouth fell open. "Have we taught you nothing?"

"That was Rocket's bike," Ratchet said with a snicker. "Bet he's madder than a bee all shook up in a jar."

"A bee in a jar?" Watts scoffed. "Who's a girl now?"

"Don't say derogatory things about the fairer sex," I declared.

"Don't worry about that," Spike said with a wink. "You're not a girl, Sloane. You're a *woman*."

The wolves burst out into laughter, the sound echoing off the walls. I snorted and shook my head.

"Thanks," I thumped him on the shoulder, "but I'm taken."

The laughter increased, and a couple of the guys began roughing one another up. The alcohol was starting to get to them, and I wondered if they'd have poor old Monroe run off his feet later. He was a vampire, but he looked like he was constantly on the edge of a heart attack.

Turning, I surveyed the garage, my gaze raking over the racks of tools, tires, and equipment. Apart from us and a few motorcycles, the place was empty. No cars were being worked on, no customers were knocking on the door, the music was off, and the telephone sat unplugged. The walls still bore the marks of the car bomb the Hollow Men had sent flying through the roller doors, and I felt the ghostly hands of Harley around my neck.

I shivered and rubbed my hands up and down my arms.

"Someone walk over your grave?" Spike asked, standing beside me.

"Yeah, I reckon." The usually noisy shop was so quiet, it was eerie. If I closed my eyes and listened hard enough, I was sure I could hear the ghosts of Fortitude wolves past coming out to play.

Taking another turn, I spotted Chaser's sleek, black motorcycle in the back corner, and I smiled.

"So that's what happened to Chaser's bike," I said. "I was wondering if he'd lost it for good."

"You got a taste now?" Spike asked with a grin.

"I felt the wind in my hair and a wave of bullets at my back," I declared. "The rush was—"

Chaser grunted, signalling his presence, and I looked up at him. He was so stealthy.

"I'll trade you a Harley Sportster for it," I said, pointing at his sexy, black motorcycle.

"It's stolen."

"So?"

"I like my motorcycle," he declared. "Get your own."

"I've never seen you ride it." I made a face and turned to Spike. "And he says he loves me."

The poor guy choked on his beer, causing the others to laugh again.

"Gasket's calling a meeting," Chaser said to the assembled wolves. The smiles faded and hands tightened around their beer cans. "Common room, now."

His tone suggested talk was going to get serious, and they knew exactly what that meant. A fight was on the horizon, and it wasn't going to be a walk in the park. It was surreal watching them turn from big teddy bears into the frightening werewolves I knew they embodied. We could laugh and joke and talk nonsense, but when it came down to it, these were wolves who'd committed crimes beyond comprehension under Marini. At least they had the chops to attempt to turn their lives around. Some people were destined to get stuck in the cycle...like Rocket and his pack.

I grasped Chaser's hand as we followed the wolves into the compound. This was it. Speeches would be made, the plan set out, and Fortitude would unite...or it would all fall apart. Obviously, we were counting on it sticking together. One last battle to win the war for forever. *Everyone's forever.*

The common room was packed as we entered. Forty burly wolves were arranged on every available surface and leaning against the walls. The air was thick with cigarette smoke and tension, causing me to cough slightly. Chaser glanced at me, then tugged me forwards through the mass of bodies.

"This is big," I heard someone say. "Something's going down."

"Yeah, it ain't good," another man replied.

"You think Gasket found the renegades?"

"Don't know, but Chaser and Sloane are back."

"Ringer said they had a shootout with Rocket."

"Seriously?"

Spotting Wren lingering in the back, I lifted a hand. She smiled as I sat on the arm of a couch next to Spike.

"You find the strangest people," the wolf said, following my gaze. "Never thought I'd see a witch helping a pack of wolves."

"I've seen a lot of strange things," I told him.

"Watchin' her cast spells... It puts the fear of God in me, Sloane." He shivered, his gaze locking on the witch across the room.

I looked him over. "You like her?"

"She's pretty, hey?"

I grinned and ruffled his hair.

"Listen up!" Gasket bellowed, breaking up our conversation.

Chaser leaned against the wall, half in the shadows, surveying the room.

"I know I've asked a lot of you these past weeks," Gasket went on. "More than I should. We've been split down the middle, forced into a civil war with wolves we once called brothers, lost good guys to their bullets, forced apart from our women... I know it's tough, but we have one last thing to do."

The room filled with angry murmurs, the tension in the air thickening.

"The Hollow Men and their *Hollow Riders* are a threat to us all," Gasket went on. "We need to be in this together, or we have no chance of beating them."

"Why should we take our fight to the Hollow Men?" Bones asked. "Our fight is with the renegades."

"Because they threatened Sloane," Gasket stated. "They threatened her, and they destroyed Chaser. Now they've got their sights on us."

"No thanks to them!" a wolf in the back shouted.

"Yeah!" someone else chimed in. "Things were fine until she showed up!"

"*Screw this.*" Chaser stood and looked at each wolf in turn. "You all know me," he said, glaring at Bones. "You know what I did for the pack. You know what I was to Marini. But you don't know who I was...or who I am." The room was so silent, I could hear each man breathe. "The stakes are higher than they've ever been. We face an organisation so dark, they put the things Marini did to shame. If we're going to trust and fight alongside each other, then you should know my story."

"Just what we need," someone muttered, "another secret past."

"Fortitude is a family," Chaser stated. "*This* Fortitude. And true family doesn't keep secrets."

I smiled up at him, proud of his strength and resolve to stand up to these men. This story wasn't about me—it never was—it was about Chaser. I was just lucky to be a part of it.

"Before I came to Fortitude, I was with the Hollow Men."

The room erupted, and several guys stood, including Ratchet.

"What?" he exclaimed. "Are you bloody serious?"

"I was with the Hollow Men," Chaser repeated, holding up his hand. "I was recruited into their ranks, but I didn't know it was King himself who'd turned me. He left me to fend for myself, to learn how to be a vampire, which was a bloody disaster. By the time he came back, I was begging him to take me in. He turned me into a monster to manipulate me into following him...and I did until I met Loretta, my wife. The woman they murdered because I went against them." Several men sat down at this, their faces turning white, and several pairs of eyes glanced at me. "I stood before King and pleaded for her life, but he killed her anyway. That's when I came out the pack, but instead of helping me, the alpha bound me to Fortitude for eternity while the Hollow Men only grew in power. For a hundred years, I killed for every alpha. I killed for Marini. I had no choice, everything was taken away from me…" Chaser glanced at me. "Until I met Sloane."

I flushed as I felt the entire pack turn and stare.

Chaser swallowed hard before he continued, "After I came to Fortitude, I let go of my humanity. I forgot about the revenge I wanted for my wife. I forgot what it felt like to have someone *care*. I relished the kill. I liked not being able to feel the pain anymore. I was broken… until Sloane put me back together." He lifted his head. "But what I do know is how to fight, so that's what I'm going to do. Now I fight for Sloane. I fight for Fortitude. And I fight, not only for her life but yours, too. The Hollow Men are going down. Rocket and the renegades are going down. And I'm going to make King suffer for what he did to my wife and for what he's threatened to do to Sloane. He's going choke on his blood, just like Loretta did."

The room was silent for so long, I couldn't tell which way things were going to fall. The mention of his affiliation with the Hollow Men had put everyone on edge, but the fire in Chaser's eyes when he vowed the ultimate revenge was chilling. I knew what he was capable of, but these men didn't. He'd kept himself apart for years, hiding his true nature, but now it was all coming out. Now they understood his magical bond with the pack…and his feelings for me.

No more secrets.

"We've tried to do it on our own, but we failed.

That's why I'm asking," he went on. "We can't take the vampires down without you."

The wolves glanced at each other as if they were deliberating telepathically. There was so much I still didn't understand about werewolf code of conduct. Fortitude was a democracy now, even though they still had an alpha, but that didn't mean they would help us because just Gasket said so.

Please, please, please... I crossed my fingers and my toes.

"Then let him choke," Hopper said, rising to his feet. "No one threatens our alpha and gets away with it."

"Let him choke," Spike said, adding his voice.

"Let the bastard choke!" Ratchet shouted.

One by one, the Fortitude Wolves stood, adding their consent, thumping their feet on the ground. I slipped my hand into Chaser's as I rose.

"Alpha?" I murmured into his ear.

He grunted and leaned into me. "That's what you are, Sloane. You may have deferred leadership, but you're alpha by rights."

I bit my bottom lip and began worrying it. I'd been hoping the wolves had forgotten about that, but it seemed no one had.

"This is the job to end all jobs," Gasket said. "The Hollow Men and their Hollow Riders are our enemies. They threaten not only our lives but the lives of those we love. That doesn't fly in our pack."

"I'll say," Ratchet drawled.

"So how are we going to take them down?" Watts asked. "They're out of our league."

"We've got an ex-Hollow Man on our crew," Hopper said, glancing at Chaser. "He's got the info, right?"

"I hope it counts for something," Chaser said. "It's been a hundred years, but I do know King is the target."

"If King is gone, someone else will take his place," Gasket said. "Then we'll be stuck in an endless war."

"So, it's not just a drive-by we're planning?" Spike groaned and rubbed his temples.

"No, it's a full-scale dismantle job," Hopper said. "Strip the shell, disconnect the battery, remove the wires and filters, drain the coolant and oil, then take out the engine."

I shot a look at Chaser, my lips curving into a grin. *Good analogy.*

"King is the key," he said, silencing the wolves. "He turned all the vampires in the Hollow Men's ranks. They're bound to him by more than blood. If he dies, then they'll do ninety-five percent of the dismantling for us."

"Like an alpha bond?" Spike asked.

I straightened up. "What's that?"

"It's a pack thing," the wolf explained. "The alpha is in control of the wolves in the pack, transferring their will onto the other wolves."

"Oh..." I murmured, understanding why everyone had seemed to be more chill now that Marini was gone. His lust for crime and violence had influenced the others and their personalities to the point they were complacent...even if they disagreed. King had created the Hollow Men with the vampire equivalent.

"We do it concurrently," Chaser said. "Go for King and hit the *Halcyon* at the same time."

"Once we start, we can't stop," Gasket said. "There's only one way to finish this for good, and it's a crap shot, but we have no other option but to dive into shark-infested waters and go for broke."

The assembled wolves muttered among one another, but at least no one got up and left. Several men looked shaken up by the prospect but they didn't lose their cool.

"What's the plan?" Watts asked. "Where do you want us?"

"Mayhem detail," Chaser said, his eyes shining with mischief I'd never seen before. *Man, it was hot.*

"Hell yeah," Spike said, fist-pumping the air.

"We need a crew to engage the Hollow Riders," Gasket said. "And a team to create chaos in the *Halcyon*."

"The casino?" Hopper asked. "That place is going to be tighter than a vir—"

"Yeah," I said, jabbing a finger at him. "It's going to be tight, you might get a taste of blood, but we need a distraction to get inside."

Gasket narrowed his eyes.

"Chaser and I are going after King," I declared. "You guys are going to strip the engine for us."

"You're going into that hole?" Stewie asked, looking shocked. He hadn't said a word until now, which showed how much he cared. It was sweet, but unnecessary.

I nodded. "Like Spike said earlier, I'm not a girl, I'm a *woman*. I want to see that son of a bitch *choke*."

The mood in the room lightened, but there was still heaviness on all our shoulders. A lot of blood was going to be shed in the upcoming days, and they were going forward with it, knowing they might never come home. There was no payment, no spoils to plunder, so why were they still here? Chaser said it earlier. Under Gasket, Fortitude had become a true family.

"Right," Gasket boomed, rising to his feet. "Get yourselves together and your head in the fight. We head out in two days."

"Two days?" I asked Chaser. "I know you said you'd need ten, but—"

"We need to hit them before they realise we're coming," he replied. "It has to be sooner rather than later."

"But the full moon—"

"Sloane, the pack's got this, okay?"

Gasket approached Chaser once all the wolves had dispersed. "I knew, but I..." He shook his head. "Thanks."

Chaser tilted his head to the side. "For?"

"Telling the truth to the pack. About who you are."

Chaser looked slightly uncomfortable as the older werewolf grasped his shoulders, but luckily, there wasn't a hug involved. I wasn't sure Chaser could handle it.

I watched the two men's bromance ignite, and I hoped to God the plan would work. For all our sakes.

CHAPTER 22

CHASER

"It's a decent plan," Gasket said as we stood to the side of the common room.

Sloane had moved off towards Wren as the wolves began talking amongst themselves.

"It's a long shot, is what it is," I drawled, crossing my arms over my chest. "The odds are against us."

"They've always been against us."

Voices began to rise around us, and I knew the pack was coming to the same conclusion. We'd been backed into a corner with little chance of escaping, and the only path we could take was the one that included bloodshed.

Whose fault was it? It was difficult to tell at this point.

Was it mine? After King murdered Loretta, I'd launched into a full-blown quest for revenge that ended badly. I rubbed my arm where the talisman was hidden. Look where that'd led me.

Or could it be Sloane's? All she'd been guilty of was being born with the ability to turn at will. She had no say over who her parents were or what she would become.

Blame could definitely be left at the feet of Anthony Marini, the late Fortitude alpha. His bloodthirsty schemes had brought the Hollow Men down on the pack, *hard*.

The more I thought about it, the more I wondered if we were all to blame in some way or another.

The sound of splintering bone cracked through the common room, silencing my inner brooding. Everyone fell silent as Spike fell to one knee, grunting in pain.

"Is he..." Sloane began as I edged in front of her.

"He's *turning*," Ratchet exclaimed.

"But the full moon is a week away," Sloane said, her eyes wide. "He shouldn't—"

"*Get out of here*," Spike rasped as his spine snapped.

Everyone took a step backwards, but it was too little, too late. His transformation accelerated and in a blink of an eye, Spike's body twisted, and the human was gone. An enormous, black and brown brindle wolf stood in his place.

"Bloody hell," Watts whispered.

Sloane stared at the wolf, her heart beating a fast, staccato rhythm, and she took a step towards him.

"Sloane, stay back." I grabbed her arm and pulled her away.

Glaring, she wrenched out of my grasp. "*No*."

The wolf growled, moving his gaze around the room. He looked confused, his hackles rising.

"You don't understand," I murmured. "He's not in control. He could hurt you."

Sloane looked bewildered for a moment, as if the thought hadn't occurred to her before, then shook her head. "No, *you* don't understand."

She faced Spike and moved towards him. Her steps were bold and unafraid. She held herself like...*like an alpha*.

The pack watched in stunned silence as she reached her hand towards Spike's snout. The wolf's eyes focused directly on her, shining intelligently as her fingers brushed his muzzle.

"Spike?" Her voice was soft, tentative. "It's okay. Don't be afraid."

The wolf growled, the sound rumbling in his throat, and bared his teeth.

"I know you're confused," she went on. "But I'm here to help you. *It's okay*."

The next minute passed more agonisingly than the last century. I watched Sloane kneel before Spike, his wolf form a hulking knot of hard muscle and his mouth full of sharp incisors. They stared at one another, her fingers brushing his muzzle, her gaze never leaving his.

Then, just as I was about to pull her back, the wolf sat on his haunches and lowered his head in submission. He let out a long sigh that seemed to break the tension in the room.

"Bloody hell, give us a scare next time, hey?" Sloane grinned and buried her fingers into the fur below Spike's ears. "There's a good boy."

The pack began to murmur as the wolf placed his paw on Sloane's knee.

I watched Spike's movements closely, ready to strike if his muscles coiled to attack, but as they sat there in the middle of the common room, I realised he was in control. It wasn't like a full moon, when the pack had to lock themselves away to contain the wild beasts within. He knew what he was doing. His human side had merged with the animal.

"What the hell just happened?" Bones asked, his face white. "He turned. *He bloody turned.*"

"And he's sitting there like a bloody lapdog," Watts added. "How the hell does that happen?"

"I thought Sloane was the only one of us who could turn whenever," Ratchet said.

"It's her," Wren said, edging through the wall of werewolves. "It's Sloane."

"What do you mean?" I demanded.

"When she became alpha, it stands to reason her abilities passed down to the pack."

I looked at Sloane and Spike, taking in how calm

the wolf was. Who knew how wolves were first created or what magic ran through their blood?

"So we're all like that now?" Watts asked. "We don't have to change on the full moon anymore?"

"Theoretically," the witch replied.

"Try changing back," Sloane said to Spike. "It took a bit to figure it out, but I managed it."

Spike edged backwards, glancing around the pack, who were all staring at him. I sensed his anxiety over being watched and narrowed my eyes. Turning was excruciating at the best of times; snapping every bone in your body in front of forty men, the alpha, and the witch I suspected he had a crush on, was a personal spectacle he didn't want to share. He had little choice, though.

Lowering his head, he closed his eyes...then he began to change. Slowly at first, then all at once—just like Sloane had done at DeLuca's cottage.

Spike collapsed to his knees, his naked chest heaving, and cursed. Bones tossed a blanket around his shoulders as Sloane knelt before him again.

"Spike?"

He scooped up the pieces of his torn T-shirt. "*Man,* I loved this shirt."

"Are you okay?" Sloane asked. "What happened?"

"I just..." He looked up at her with wide eyes. "I was just thinking about it."

She nodded and rubbed her palm over his shoulder. "That's all it seemed to take when I transformed for the first time." Her gaze moved to mine. "I willed it and it happened."

"You haven't noticed any changes?" I asked the wolves. "Strength, smell, that sort of thing?"

"Honestly, we've been pretty flat-out," Rhodes told me. "I know I haven't had time to scratch my—"

"Watch it," Spike hissed, glancing at Wren. "There're ladies present."

The wolves scoffed and began laughing, jostling him.

"This changes everything," I said to Gasket as the pack teased Spike. "We don't have to rely on the full moon."

"We'll have an edge over Rocket and the renegades," the old wolf murmured. "But we need to test this theory. If we can turn when we want, it may be the twist that wins the battle."

"Don't forget the Hollow Men," Sloane reminded us. "The fight will be more evenly matched."

I nodded and looked around at the pack. They seemed excited, the prospect at not having to transform on the full moon was a dream come true... but adjusting to a new ability this close to an all-out war...? It made a dicey situation even more tenuous.

"Be careful," I warned Gasket. "It's a blessing, but it could also be a curse."

The old wolf nodded, his forehead creasing. "Bloody oath, don't I know it."

CHAPTER 23

SLOANE

I laid on my bed, staring at the ceiling. Glad for the moment of silence, I thought about everything that'd happened that day.

My head spun with the plan Gasket and Chaser had cooked up and with Spike's unexpected transformation.

I'd knelt before him, my hands in his fur, and I'd felt... I didn't know. Powerful? At peace?

His wolf eyes were full of human understanding, and I *knew* he was in control. The whole werewolf thing was still new to me, and the alpha part was a complete mystery.

If they could control their transformations, then they wouldn't have to go through all that pain every full moon. They would have a *choice*.

It was a big deal, and I wondered what that meant for me and for Gasket's position as stand-in alpha.

Chaser was right about that part—I killed Marini, so I was top wolf until someone came and knocked me off my pedestal. After what happened with Spike, I'd probably be on the throne for life.

Sighing, I rubbed my eyes. There had to be magic involved. Magic seemed to have touched everything in the supernatural world and held it all together, forming connections I didn't think I'd ever understand.

I lifted my head at the sound of knocking at my door. "Yeah?"

It creaked open and Wren's blonde head appeared. "Is this a good time?"

I sat up and gestured for her to come in. "I'm sorry, Gasket said something about you wanting to talk to me. It's been so crazy..."

"That's okay," the witch said, hugging a leather-bound book against her chest. "Is it always a mad house around here?"

I shrugged. "In the couple of weeks I've been here, sure. But I think it's all been one big, isolated incident."

She closed the door and sat beside me. "Today was unexpected."

"God, the last thing I thought would've happened at that meeting was a spontaneous wolf transformation," I replied. "Do you really think they've inherited my abilities?"

"Sure. They'll need to verify it on the next full moon, but Spike transforming like that... I'm fairly certain they can control their werewolf sides, but they'll need to be careful. Otherwise, it'd be quite the sight to see a person change into a wolf at the local supermarket."

"I'll say," I said with a snort. "What's that you've got there?"

"Actually, that's why I'm here." Wren set her hands on top of the book. "I wanted to show you something."

"The book?"

"It's called a grimoire." She opened the cover, the spine cracking, and leafed through the pages. "It contains all the spells and knowledge passed down through my coven from the witch who created it."

I stared at it with interest. It must be the spell book Gasket had mentioned.

Spidery writing and strange symbols filled the discoloured pages, and I gazed at it in interest. I didn't understand any of it, but all the runes, sigils, and drawings looked magical enough. Some reminded me of old alchemy formulas and zodiac charts I'd seen on artwork hanging in new age stores. These had actual practical applications, though.

"How old is it?" I asked.

"This one was started by an ancestor in the 1800s. She brought it to Australia from England. Something about escaping witch trials."

I raised my eyebrows. "In the 1800s?"

"Sure. The hysteria was long over, but there was still persecution amongst real supernaturals. I guess she wanted to start a new life away from all that."

Wren ran her fingers over a detailed page, tracing the inked words. "This is the spell I wanted to talk to you about."

"What does it do?"

"This is the ritual."

My expression faded. I didn't know what to say. Wren had access to the ritual King was so desperate to perform? I blinked. *Of course, she did.* Her coven had *written it.* "Your ancestor..."

"It was her attempt to reverse engineer the spell that created the first vampires," she explained. "It wasn't intended for King or his plans to become immortal because it's not quite right for that."

"There's something wrong with it?"

"King wants true immortality, right?" I nodded and she continued, "But he's already a vampire. This spell was intended for a human. *A mortal.* I can see how everyone missed it...it took me a long time to figure it out."

I frowned. "So, it won't work?"

"Oh, it'll work," Wren told me, "but I don't think it'll end up exactly how he planned."

"What do you mean?"

"The ritual, as written, needs the blood of a founding vampire—one of the first, but apparently, there are none left..."

"That's why they want to substitute mine?"

"Yeah, and that's the problem. Instead of creating another founding vampire—a true immortal that can't be killed—I think they're going to create a hybrid instead. Half-vampire, half—"

"Wolf," I whispered.

"Unless there's some twist I haven't foreseen. Maybe the quirk that separates your blood from regular werewolves is the binding agent they need to separate King's blood from his vampirism..." She shook her head. "If I had more time, maybe I could figure it out."

"So, it's a fifty-fifty chance," I mused. "I don't care to know which."

"Me neither, but if it comes down to it, his shock may be the moment you or Chaser need to finish him. There's also one other thing..."

I groaned. "There's always another thing, isn't there?"

"This one isn't *that* bad." She looked down at the spell again. "They don't need to kill you to complete the ritual. All they need is some of your blood, not all of it."

"*You're kidding me.*"

Wren shook her head. "You don't have to die, Sloane, but King will kill you anyway to make sure no one else can use you against him."

It was a sick joke, but by this point in the whole mess, I wasn't actually that surprised.

"Then we have to make sure we win tomorrow," I murmured, my heart heavy.

Wren closed the grimoire and tried her best to

smile reassuringly. "I thought you deserved to know everything. To be prepared."

"I'd feel better if you came with us, but it's too dangerous. Chaser and I understand what we're getting into, but I can't ask you to risk any more than you already have." She'd lost her entire family to the Hollow Men. As the last of her coven, I knew her life was precious—bloodlines and all that. "Thanks for being honest."

"I'll be there tomorrow," she told me after a moment. "There isn't much I can do against a whole coven, but if I can help, I'll be ready."

I felt tears prickling in my eyes, and I pulled her in for a hug before she could see them.

"Thank you," I murmured as she embraced me. "*Thank you.*"

Tomorrow night.

I stared at my reflection in my bathroom mirror, hardly recognising the woman looking back at me. The last few months had taken their toll, shedding weight from my body and replacing some of it with muscle. Whoever she was, she looked tough. Toned, dangerous, determined.

Betty was gone. Sloane was gone. So, who was I now? I was Sloane, Mark II.

My stomach churned as I thought about our plan.

Would I have the guts to pull the trigger if I came face-to-face with King? This wasn't like facing my father. This was that moment in the bush, amplified times a million. This was the end game.

I swallowed hard. Yeah, I could do it, and it had nothing to do with pulling a trigger. I would take King down any way possible. *He deserves it.* I was taking his game, turning it back on him, and shoving the ragged remains right up his backside. *See how you like it, then.*

One way or another, in twenty-four hours, everything was going to change.

The door opened and Chaser appeared, moving silently across the room. He leaned against the doorjamb and crossed his arms over his chest.

I narrowed my eyes at him in the mirror. "How's Spike?"

"He's pretty pleased with himself," the vampire replied. "He can control his wolf now *and* remember."

"I never knew that," I murmured.

"What?"

"That they couldn't remember what they did while in their wolf form." I sighed, recalling what it was like the first night I'd turned out on the Nullarbor. "I remember everything. I was myself, but I wasn't." I frowned. "It's strange...I can't find the right words to describe it."

"You were the wolf."

I looked up at Chaser and nodded. "I suppose I could control it because of my abilities."

"And now you've passed them to the pack."

I turned and wiped my palms on my thighs.

"You look uncomfortable."

"A little. I spent most of my life hiding, and now it's like I'm their saviour. I saved them from their curse."

"That's exactly what you did," Chaser told me.

"It's a supernatural loophole."

"Even so, it's a welcomed one. How's planning going with Gasket?"

"He's delegated men to each team," I replied. "Bones, Hopper, Stewie, Ringer, and Davis are on mayhem duty at the *Halcyon*. The rest are going with Gasket to confront Rocket. Seems like the Hollow Riders have taken up residence in a certain diner." I air quoted the renegades shitty new name and curled my lip in distaste.

"*Monroe's*?"

I nodded. "He isn't very happy since he still owns the place."

"Obviously."

"He'll get it back," I murmured, checking my hair in the mirror. "We'll all get back what we've lost."

"To a certain extent."

I looked at Chaser's reflection in the mirror and held in my sigh. We didn't need this right now. Strength was in short supply, and we had to gather all we could find for the climax.

I frowned. "Are you okay?"

"I feel...raw," he murmured.

"You're evolving, too," I whispered. "Stings like a bitch, doesn't it?"

His lips twitched. "Everything's progressing on schedule," he said, avoiding the question. "All we have to do is wait until tomorrow."

I moved past him, stepping inside the bedroom and sitting on the bed. Suddenly, I felt weak in the knees. The air was so heavy with the incoming storm that all I wanted to do was grab Chaser and never let go. I wanted to draw him into a little cocoon and stay there forever. Just him and me.

He sat beside me, his arm circling my waist. Just his touch was enough to send a bolt of longing into my heart.

"What do you hope for, Chaser?"

"You want to know about my hopes and dreams?" he asked with a laugh. "Shit."

"Yeah. So?"

He grunted.

"This has to do with after. We've talked about it, but not seriously," I said. "So, let's make a concrete plan, something to get us through the next couple of days. Something to look forward to."

Chaser lowered his gaze and picked up my hand. Rubbing his fingers over mine, he nodded. "You go first."

"I want to go see Yvette," I said. "I want to see how Sam's doing. Besides, I made her a promise."

"You did?"

"Yeah. I told her if I ever got through to the other side of this, I'd let her know. I want to let her know. In person."

"Okay," he agreed. "We go there first."

"What about you?"

He thought for a moment, his brow creasing with the effort. "Can I ask you something?"

"Sure."

"When you left foster care, why did you pick Perth?"

"Honestly? It was the farthest place away from here. There wasn't any deep or powerful meaning. I just wanted to run far, far away." I studied his expression but got nothing. "Are you disappointed?"

"No."

"Chaser, I... I never belonged anywhere before, not really."

He cupped my cheek. "It doesn't matter where we go as long as we're together."

I grinned. "See? I said you were getting soft. Like a big, squishy teddy bear."

"Bloody hell," he groaned and rolled his eyes. "What did I say about ruining my reputation?"

"Am I denting your fragile male ego?"

"No. I'm too hard for that."

I laughed and fell back onto the bed, but the moment faded as soon as my head hit the mattress.

"It's a fantasy, isn't it?" I murmured, staring at the celling.

"What is?"

"All this talk about after. Our life together...just you and me. I'm the Fortitude alpha. I gave my gift to the pack and if I bow to Gasket, there's a chance I'll take it from them. They'll be forced to turn in agony on every full moon again."

"Nothing's certain."

"I can't take that from them," I whispered.

"I know," Chaser said, kissing my forehead. "Whatever you decide, know that I'll be here with you."

I gazed up at him, my heart swelling. Gone was the abrasive, cold vampire I'd met at the *Sailor's Arms* in Fremantle, and here was the human who'd once walked the streets of London—William Mason, the stonemason working on the Tower Bridge. The man who'd broken free of the Hollow Men. The man who'd fallen in love with a human woman and was forced to watch as the light left her eyes.

Whatever happened tomorrow night, I wouldn't let him see me die.

CHAPTER 24

SLOANE

I was a ball of nervous energy the following day.

My mind was full of the wolves' new abilities, Wren's discovery, and the imminent firestorm at the *Halcyon*. After all this time—after the attacks, death threats, and struggles—I was going to come face-to-face with King himself. The vampire who wanted to sacrifice me in a twisted blood ritual to make himself the last true immortal to walk the Earth.

Allegedly.

Dressing, we gathered our bags and triple-checked our guns and ammo before making our way down to the garage. Everyone was assembled, waiting for the word to move out. For better or worse, today was going to be a big day in the history of the Fortitude Wolves.

"This is how it's going down," Gasket said, nodding to acknowledge our arrival. "We ride for the city in half an hour. Mayhem crew—you'll hold tight until seven, after which, you'll enter the casino from separate entrances. Head inside, gamble, drink, make noise. Make that security team work for it. My crew—we'll stake out *Monroe's* and watch their comings and goings. We'll need to play it by ear. If they leave, we'll need to follow. At seven sharp, we'll strike, no matter where they are. Got it?"

The wolves nodded their agreement.

"Whatever happens tonight, the Hollow Riders will be in the ground," he added. "No excuses. Restrain those who want to bow to Sloane and show no mercy for those who don't, because they'll show none for you."

"Sloane and I will enter the *Halcyon* just after seven," Chaser said, eyeing the mayhem crew made up of Bones, Hopper, Stewie, Ringer, Watts, and Davis. "We're counting on you to be our smoke screen."

"Things might get rough without warning," I said. "You'll need to be ready to make things up on the fly."

"We've got your back," Hopper said with a nod. "Don't worry about us. You worry about getting the big man."

"Then saddle up," Gasket said. "You know the plan. Stick to it."

The wolves began to move, gathering their stuff, and the garage filled with the noise of mobilisation.

"Take care of yourself, kid," Gasket said.

"Don't get yourself killed," I replied, throwing my

arms around him. "I expect to see you tomorrow, okay?"

"Same here." He sniffed, his voice wavering.

"Are you crying?" I pulled back and made a face.

"No way."

I saw his eyes sparkling, and I laughed. "Liar."

"I'll see you tomorrow. Free and clear, okay?"

I nodded and smoothed down his vest. "Courage in pain and adversity."

"And you, kid." He stepped back, raising a fist. "Fortitude! Let's ride!"

The assembled werewolves sprang into action and filed out the roller door. We followed, wishing them luck as we went.

We lingered on the pavement as the entire pack powered up their motorcycles and formed a convoy on the street. One by one, they moved off, their engines roaring as they departed. It was a hell of a sight.

"That's not exactly inconspicuous," I said, plugging my ears. Marini had styled the pack into a motorcycle club, and it pained me to see it.

"They know what they're doing," Chaser replied, pulling the car keys from his pocket. "This isn't their first rumble."

I knew these were seasoned men, but it didn't help knowing they were en route to a bloodbath. When Gasket said they would deal with the Hollow Riders, he meant kill them. But who was I to fret over it? We were going to kill King and anyone else who got in our way—our forever depended on it.

"So many things could go wrong with this," I said, feeling nauseous. I didn't even know where Wren was stationed—she'd left the compound hours ago—but I supposed that was the point.

"And so many things can go right," Chaser replied.

I took a deep breath and held it for a second. Finally, I let it out like I was letting go of the last shred of fear and doubt I'd been holding on to.

"Are you ready?" Chaser asked.

"Ready as I'll ever be."

I leaned back in my chair and sighed. I felt sick. The nervous kind of sick that made me want to rush to the bathroom and stay there.

I could see the spiked tower of the *Halcyon* rising towards the sky in the distance. We kept a few blocks between us, waiting for go-time. We hadn't heard from Gasket or the mayhem crew, but I knew we wouldn't until the operation was over. I wondered if that was what made me so queasy, but knowing Wren was out there somewhere, watching over us, was comforting.

I turned my attention to the street in front of us. We'd chosen a little café to wait at, ordering some food and drinks, and sat at an outside table hidden in a corner. From here, we could see the comings and goings of the restaurant and watch the foot traffic.

It felt strange sitting on one of the most populated streets in Melbourne with a thousand and one security cameras and police officers around us, knowing that they may or may not be in the Hollow Men's back pocket—compelled or not.

I pushed my sunglasses up my nose and glanced at the sky. The sun was starting to go down.

I was also getting used to the constant furnace that the sun and the glass and concreted city created. I didn't even notice the under-boob sweat anymore. *Typical.* The moment we get to the crescendo, I finally learn to deal with the heat.

Chaser glanced at his watch.

"What's the time?" I asked.

"Six-forty."

"I need to go to the toilet," I said with a groan.

"That's just nerves."

"Sexy, huh?" I smiled in an attempt to alleviate some of the churning in my small bowel.

"Sunset is seven-oh-five," he said, his lips quirking. *Not infallible to toilet humour...noted.* "We'll move then."

"Okay."

"You got everything?"

I felt the weight of the revolver press into the small of my back, hidden by the oversized T-shirt I'd donned that morning. It wasn't exactly a tactical outfit, but tonight wasn't about fashion. We needed to blend in until we got to the upper floors of the *Halcyon*. Then it wouldn't matter.

Nodding, I brushed my fingers over the other Glock I had hidden at my waist. The revolver only held six bullets, so additional firepower was a must. If it weren't for the symbolic justice my father's gun represented, I would've just brought the one.

"This'll go fast," he said. "Whatever you do, don't stop walking, okay?"

"I won't."

We rose from the table, and Chaser tossed a couple of notes down, setting an empty glass over them so they wouldn't blow away. Taking my hand, he led me out onto the street, and we walked the two blocks to the *Halcyon* in silence.

At this stage, we'd said everything that needed to be said. We'd made our plans, said what was in our hearts, and shed all our fears. This was the moment we'd been working towards since the moment we met. Revenge, justice...it was a little of both.

We were one step away from forever.

"Keep your head down," Chaser said. "The cameras won't be able to get a clear picture that way."

"Do you think they've got facial recognition?"

"Probably."

Following Chaser's advice, I lowered my head, and we walked hand-in-hand into the casino. A few clothing boutiques, a lingerie store, and several restaurants filled the immediate foyer. Then the pokies began to take over. Rows upon rows of flashing lights and electronic beeps assaulted our eyes as we were jostled by thousands of gamblers elbowing to find the perfect machine. I saw one lady kiss each dollar coin before she put it into an Ancient Egyptian-themed machine, and I wished that winning the jackpot was the most of my worries.

When we made it to the main gaming floor, we glanced towards the mass of roulette tables and caught a glimpse of a scuffle erupting between staff and a few men. Security guards were rushing over, shouting and talking into their walkie-talkies. Someone picked up a chair and flung it, the metal crashing into a table, sending chips flying. Chaser grasped my arm and tugged me in the opposite direction as a brawl erupted.

The mayhem crew was coming through.

"Head down," he murmured as two vampires sprinted past us. They didn't even glance our way as they rushed to break up the fight, which was getting louder by the second.

I glimpsed Hopper in the distance, who bolted down a row of slot machines to join in the madness.

Finally, we made it to the foyer of the hotel and stood in front of the bank of elevators. I pressed the call button, and the revolver felt heavy against my back as we waited. When an elderly couple stood near us, I swallowed hard. There was no way they would know who we were, but I didn't like lingering. I glanced at them out the corner of my eye, but they weren't even looking at us. They were watching for the elevator.

A ding signalled a car had arrived, and a set of doors swished open to our right. A few people exited, laughing and chattering, and didn't bother looking at us. Sniffing, I deduced they were human guests headed out for the evening.

I darted into the elevator, keeping my head angled towards the floor. There were cameras in here, likely in the ceiling, but I wasn't looking up to find out.

The elderly couple went to step into the elevator with us, and Chaser held up his hand. "This one's taken."

I jammed my finger on the close button as they blinked at us in confusion. He'd used his vampiric mind-control for the first time in my presence, and the ease of it made me do a double-take.

The doors slid shut, and we were alone. Those old folks had no idea they were staying at a hotel owned by a maniacal vampire—no one did—and Chaser just demonstrated how easy it was to dupe the lot of them.

He pressed the button for the penthouse, but it wouldn't light up.

"I think we need a keycard," I murmured. "Unless it's a magic thing."

Chaser grunted and pressed the button for the floor below it. The button shone red, and we began to rise.

"How are we going to get up there? You don't

expect me to scale the..." I shut my mouth, suddenly anxious the cameras had ears, too.

"Hopefully, there's someone I can stake who has one," Chaser replied. "I doubt I'd be able to force the elevator door open from inside the shaft, anyway. There's a reason we haven't crossed any magical wards." They were all upstairs, guarding the king of the perverted castle.

I swallowed hard and watched the numbers on the display go up. When we reached thirty-three, the car came to a stop, and the doors slid open. Peering down the hall beyond, Chaser gestured for me to follow. The plush beige carpet muffled our footsteps as we moved forwards, but the décor was otherwise bland and uninspiring. The long line of hotel room doors were closed, and nothing moved. I couldn't hear a sound other than our movements.

The whole place smelt strange, like metallic-tinged pine disinfectant. Someone had done some serious cleaning. *Blood*, I realised. *They'd been erasing evidence.*

"I can't hear anything," I whispered. "But this place *reeks*."

Chaser glanced at me. "It's a nest."

"A *what?*"

"Let's just say vampires living together in large quantities isn't a good thing."

A wave of uneasiness came over me, and I reached for the Glock under my shirt. What the hell was this place?

We moved on, rounding a corner. More rooms and another empty hallway, though at the end was a glowing exit sign.

"This is too easy," I said. "I expected there to be vampires...lots of them."

Chaser grimaced, and I knew he was thinking the same thing. Up until now, the Hollow Men had always been one step ahead of us. They knew what we were doing before we even thought to do it. Something was wrong. We shouldn't have been able to get this far without a hotel keycard.

"We can't go back now," he said. "This is our one chance. We'll have to play it by ear."

I nodded and tightened my grip on the revolver. The only way left open to us was straight ahead.

"Try another hall?" I offered.

Chaser nodded, and we went back the way we came. The moment we turned the corner, we stopped in our tracks, and my heart twisted and stopped beating. I literally died for a full thirty seconds as everything came crashing down. I didn't believe it when people said their lives flashed before their eyes in a near-death moment. I still didn't believe it because nothing happened when I saw my mortality staring at me down the barrel of several guns.

A group of male vampires blocked our way, their guns pointed directly at us. Behind them, several hotel room doors were open. I turned, only to find more had emerged from rooms in the hall we'd just been in.

Ambushed.

"We really suck at this," I said, raising my hands. "Like epically."

Chaser grunted. What else was he supposed to say during a moment like this?

We were screwed.

CHAPTER 25
SLOANE

We were dragged into the *Halcyon*'s penthouse at gunpoint, all our hopes bursting into flames.

The main living room stretched out before us, the space filled with leather sofas, expensive art on the walls, plush carpets, and floor-to-ceiling windows that showed a panoramic view of the Melbourne skyline. If it weren't for our imminent deaths, it would've been almost pretty with all the twinkling lights.

Two men waited for us in the middle of the expanse...one of them was King himself.

As my gaze met his, I only felt one thing. *Cold.* His black stare chilled me right to my core; the absolute power he held was like a knife to my very soul.

Psychopath.

King smiled at me, basking in his triumph. His silver-streaked hair was swept back in a fancy quiff, his beard short and clipped to perfection. He wore an expensive-looking slate-grey suit, his black shirt undone at the collar. Silver cufflinks glinted as he straightened his sleeves, preening for his audience.

The man standing next to him was rougher around the edges. He had a mean look about him—pinched lips and cold eyes—and I knew he was just as awful as King. I had a bad feeling he was here to cause pain...a lot of it.

"You remember Sloss," King said, smiling at Chaser. "He was disappointed he didn't get to spend more time with you."

The vampire beside him grinned, his lip curling sadistically.

"If you hurt him—" The man holding me tightened his grip, twisting my wrists until pain shot up both arms.

"What you see in him, I'll never know." King prowled forwards, and I jerked away from him, but I was yanked back again. "Tell me, Sloane, what would it take for you to forget him? Money? Power? Or perhaps the freedom of your pack?"

Oh God, Gasket. They knew the pack was going after the Hollow Riders. They knew about the mayhem crew downstairs in the casino. Were they already dead?

No, I thought. *They're smarter than that.* King couldn't know they'd inherited my power. I had to believe they were fine. I had to believe they'd win.

"You can't put a price on life," I snarled. "And you especially can't put it on love."

King let out a laugh, and on cue, his entourage of armed heavies joined in. The result was an empty charade of what this vampire's life had become. He didn't know love. These men would kill for him, but not because they cared for the guy. It may have begun as a supernatural manipulation—King 'saved' them from their terrible fates—but it had morphed into a situation they all profited from. It was about blood and power. *Immortality*. They were as sadistic as he was.

"Love?" His eyebrows rose. "Love is a farce, Sloane. The sooner you realise it, the sooner you'll be happy."

"A thousand years on this Earth and you're still as dumb as the day you were born," I spat at him.

It only took a split-second for his expression to change from amusement to complete darkness. He raised his hand and struck me across the face, his knuckles rapping the side of my mouth. His ring dragged against my skin, splitting my lip. My head fell to the side and my vision blurred.

"Bastard!" Chaser roared.

I tasted blood on my tongue as Chaser's legs were kicked out from beneath him, forcing him to his knees. There was nothing I could do.

"As you now realise," King began as my flesh began to heal, "you now belong to me. *Both of you*. You can't fight. You'll never win, so you can save yourselves a lot of pain by coming to terms with that fact. Simple, no?" He eyed both of us.

"You killed Loretta," Chaser snarled. "You shot her in the throat and forced me to watch her choke. I'll never give up."

"Oh no, I didn't just shoot her," he said. "She cried and cried while I had my fun. It was quite pitiful, actually."

Chaser pushed upwards but was forced back onto his knees.

"How does that make you feel, Sloane?" King asked me. "Knowing how your pretty boyfriend still pines for his wife after a hundred years? Do you think he loves you like he loves her?"

"You can never turn us against each other," Chaser snarled.

The vampire tilted his head to the side and regarded us thoughtfully. Nothing moved for a full minute as he silently deliberated.

"Take him," King said, waving a hand at Chaser. "Put him in the other bedroom and give him what he asked for."

The men holding Chaser pulled him away, and I thrashed against the heavy who was grasping my arm with brute force.

"No!" I screeched. "Don't touch him!"

"Take the wolf into the other room," King went on. "And get the witches."

I gasped, realising he meant to perform the ritual

tonight. "No." I pulled against the hands holding me. "No, I won't let you!"

King absently waved at me, ignoring my pleas.

A second man came forwards and grabbed hold of me, and I was dragged into the next room, kicking and screaming. I was slapped across the face, then my arms were wrenched in front, and a man bound each wrist with thick nylon cord, leaving some slack in between.

Finally, they lifted me and looped the rope around a hook that hung from the ceiling, my weight causing the bindings to drag painfully at my wrists. My toes barely touched the ground, so I felt no relief. I was strung up like a carcass in a butcher's refrigerator, unable to do anything but swing.

Desperate, I pulled against the rope, my gaze burning with hatred for the vampire standing with his back to me. All I had to do was turn and I could tear him apart right now. All I had to do was *will it*.

I called out to the wolf inside me, praying to the moon that this would work...but nothing happened. A frustrated cry tore from my lips and I kicked out at the vampires who'd strung me up, but they easily dodged my feet.

The rope was spelled to bind my wolf. There was no other explanation.

"Leave us," King said, gesturing to the two vampires. My struggles went unnoticed, and I knew I was in trouble. "Make sure the witches aren't hindered."

"Sir?" They seemed hesitant.

"I said, *leave us.*"

I saw the fear in their eyes as they backed out of the room, closing the door behind them. It was a modest space, though the furnishings were premium. A king-sized bed took up much of the room, and floor-to-ceiling windows stretched across one side, revealing a spectacular view of the Melbourne city skyline beyond.

King breathed in deeply, air whistling through his nostrils. "Alone at last."

I tensed, pursing my lips. I couldn't let him get into my head. I had to clear my mind and work out how to get out of this. If I could get down, then I had a chance. Not much of one, but it was better than letting King sacrifice me.

"After all these years," he murmured, raking his fingers through my hair. I jerked my head to the side, but he grabbed a chunk and pulled.

"Enjoy this moment," I said, seething. "Enjoy it while it lasts, you sick son of a bitch, because it will be the last time."

He smiled and leaned closer, breathing deeply.

Bile rose in the back of my throat, signalling terror was attempting to claw its way to the surface. *I wouldn't let it.*

"What did you think you were going to do, Sloane? Break into my penthouse and stake me?"

"You know what we were going to do," I retorted. "Stop playing your games."

A pained cry tore through the wall separating me from Chaser, and my heart twisted. The awful sounds of flesh hitting flesh were muffled but unmistakable. Their 'warm welcome' was nothing more than a glorified beating.

I swung, my shoulders aching as I was forced to hear Chaser in pain. Staring defiantly at my captor, I imagined blowing a hole in his head, right between his eyes.

King's lips quirked as the sounds intensified. "He held out longer than I thought he would. They usually scream within the first thirty seconds." He stood before me and his smile widened. "That feeling you have now…? William is going to be lying there, covered in his own blood, listening to your screams as my witches sacrifice you."

I glanced around the room, looking for a way out.

"Escape is futile," he said, watching me. "The rope is spelled to contain your transformation. You're little more than a fragile human, Sloane. It's over; save yourself the pain of struggling and *submit*."

"*Never*."

The door opened behind him and four women walked in, their gazes blank. *The witches.*

"This will be painful," King told me. "Try not to scream, little wolf. It will be over soon."

The witches filed past the vampire, arranging

themselves around me. They took their places—north, south, east, and west—and knelt.

If I didn't do anything, there wouldn't be a happy ending for me or the pack. I would be dead, sacrificed to create whatever King was about to become—immortal or hybrid, the jury was still out as to which. I winced as the sounds of Chaser being beaten in the next room intensified. I bit my lip, stifling my tears.

The witches began to chant, their magic filling the room with a metallic tang that coated my tongue. King stood before me, his grin as wide as his outstretched arms.

Remember what Chaser taught you, I thought. *Remember. Freedom, love, forever.*

I fought against the magic binding me, willing the wolf to come forwards. No magic could hold me. I was the wolf who could change at will. The moon was my friend, my confidant, my familiar. No curse bound me, no magic could contain the wolf within.

Love was stronger than any spell.

"Freedom, love, *forever*..." I whispered.

Pain ripped through my body as my bones shattered. My limbs twisted into legs, my hands morphed into paws, my back splintered, and my jaws twisted.

My wolf legs slipped free of the ropes binding me and I landed on the carpet, growling as King stared down at me in shock.

The witches fell silent, their fear thick in the air,

but there was something else...blood. The sickly scent of blood trickling in from underneath the door. *Chaser.*

I let go, giving control to the wolf and I attacked, leaping at the first body I could find. My jaws clamped down of flesh, tearing, biting, twisting. I tasted blood as I turned and followed the sound of each beating heart. I hunted them as they'd hunted me.

No magic touched me. No curse bound me. No force contained me.

Freedom, love, forever.

Hands clamped down on my neck and threw me across the room. I collided with the wall, but I landed on my feet in time to leap again. I collided with King, my jaws closing around his neck, and I tore.

The vampire fell to the floor, gurgling as blood spurted out of his throat. It coated his shirt and pooled around his body, gushing and flowing freely.

I stood over him with my teeth bared and watched as the light left his eyes. His body couldn't heal fast enough to stop the bleeding. This was the end of a thousand years of terror. There was no stake, no torn-out heart...just a slow, painful drowning in his own filth.

King's fingers grazed the tip of my bloodied paw, then he went slack, his eyes glazing over.

Then...

The blood bubbled through the hole in his throat as the desiccation creeped up towards his face.

And then it took over, the life wasting away and leaving nothing but a withered corpse behind.

King was dead.

Thank you, I thought, leaping over his desiccated remains. *Thank you for showing me how powerful I really am. I'll never forget it.*

CHAPTER 26

CHASER

Blood dripped from my mouth and soaked into the carpet.

A fist slammed into the back of my head, and I fell facedown, my ribs burning. A boot collided with my side, and despite biting my tongue, I cried out. I was pummelled, punched, and kicked savagely, and when I healed, it began all over again.

But all I could think about was Sloane. I had to get to her, I—

I roared in pain as Sloss stomped on my arm. He laughed and went on kicking. My head snapped to the side as a boot collided with the side of my face, stars exploding through my vision.

"I'll kill you," I rasped.

"Hear that?" the vampire mocked. "He says he's going to kill us."

The second vampire burst out laughing and slapped Sloss on the shoulder. "Like to see him try."

"I'll kill you," I said again.

"No, you won't," Sloss said, his eyes changing colour. "You won't have the chance."

Resignation filled every pore of my body as I realised this was probably my last stand. Sloss wasn't a vampire; he was something else, a weapon King should have used the first time I'd come to the *Halcyon*.

"You're not a vampire," I whispered.

"Oh, I'm a vampire," Sloss said, smiling. "But I'm something else, too." He grasped my shredded arm, his touch sending metallic fire through my veins. "I distinctly remember you asking King to remove the magic binding you to the werewolves. I'm here to make sure your wish is granted."

I roared in pain as he ripped the flesh away from my bones, exposing the talisman Wren had implanted. The fire spread and I felt the magic bleed from my body and into Sloss. *What the hell was he?*

Then there was a bang at the door, and it flung inwards, revealing a snarling, blood-splattered wolf.

Sloane.

Before the vampires could react, she leapt, slamming into their chests, her jaws snapping and tearing in a shower of blood. The first vampire dropped and Sloss stumbled and reached for his gun, but Sloane was faster. She was on him in a flash, her jaws clamping savagely around his neck, and he went down.

Screams mixed with guttural growls, and the smell of blood intensified. I couldn't lift my head to see what was happening, and I gasped as I tried to reach my good arm towards the wolf.

"Sloane..."

A human woman fell to her knees beside me, her mouth falling open in shock. *It must be bad, then.*

Sloane was drenched in blood, but beneath it, her injuries were clear. Her wrists were rubbed raw and bleeding, her lip was split, and a red mark blazed across her cheek.

"He hung you," I said, my fingers weakly brushing against her wrists. "The bastard hung you."

"Past tense," she murmured, checking my wounds —hers were already healing. "I tore him apart." She paused, her gaze meeting mine. "I tore out his throat and made sure he knew."

"He choked."

"He choked."

"Good." I closed my eyes, but everything burned. I was fairly sure I had cracked ribs, a shredded arm, a severe concussion—all of which should have healed by now.

"Oh, God," Sloane whispered, realising how bad I was.

I could feel it. The coldness seeped into my veins,

spreading across my chest and into my limbs. I was dying for real this time.

"The talisman—"

"The talisman's magic is gone," I rasped. "Sloss had magic. He—" I rolled onto my back and gritted my teeth as my broken bones grated. Nausea rolled through my stomach, and I swallowed to keep myself from throwing up.

"Just so you know, this is the complete opposite of Thelma and Louise." Sloane smoothed the hair from my brow.

I coughed, my ribs grating together. The desiccation was slow, but I knew that was the point. King had wanted me to suffer.

A tear fell from her eye and her bloodied hands found mine. "What do we do?" she said, her voice breaking. "I don't know what to do."

"End it," I whispered.

"*What?*" Her eyes shimmered, her wolf still simmering underneath the surface.

"Take a stake and put it through my heart."

Her hands began to tremble, and she shook her head. "No... *No.*"

"Sloane," I managed to say, "it's for real this time."

Her gaze searched mine and there was a sudden change. "We can do the ritual," she murmured. "You don't have to die."

"*No.*" I coughed, tasting blood. "I won't let you die for me."

"No, no, no..." She smoothed her hand over my cheek. "Wren told me all about it. I never had to die, Chaser. It was only my blood they needed. King just wanted to cover his tracks."

"I don't want to live forever if I can't be with you."

"You won't be immortal," she whispered, her tears flowing freely. "King had it all wrong. They all did. You won't be a true immortal, you'd be... You'd be half-wolf."

"How...?" I couldn't imagine it. After a century bound to the Fortitude Wolves, the thought of becoming one wasn't a concept that'd crossed my mind. No magic could create a beast like that. It was false hope.

But Sloane seemed to believe it. "Wren can help you. *I trust her.*"

The coldness was spreading, and I couldn't feel my feet anymore.

"I won't force it on you," she went on, her hands exploring every part of my face, her touch gentle. "I won't do the same thing King did. If you want it—" She choked back a sob. "It's your choice."

"*Sloane...*"

"Just make me a promise, okay? Don't do it for me. Do it for *yourself*. I will love you no matter what."

The door burst open, breaking us apart, and Sloane pushed to her feet, snarling.

The five werewolves on the mayhem crew came barging in—Bones, Hopper, Stewie, Ringer, and Davis

—and came to a sudden halt when they saw Sloane. Their eyes widened, but none of them had anything to say.

We must have looked quite the sight. Surrounded by dismembered bodies, their alpha naked and covered in blood, and me, my arm torn open, exposing the bones within, slowly desiccating before their eyes.

"Get Wren," Sloane shouted at the wolves. "*Get her now!*"

CHAPTER 27
SLOANE

It was midnight when we arrived at the remains of DeLuca's cottage.

The plot of land was the only site we knew that was remote and safe enough for the ritual. And if Chaser decided against it, a peaceful place underneath the stars where we could spend our final moments together.

The bush was silent, cast in a silver glow from the almost full moon. It hung high, watching over us as Stewie and Bones laid Chaser down on a patch of grass.

I stood by Wren and the wolves, my entire body numb. I was wearing Hopper's shirt, the hem long enough to cover all the important bits, but I didn't care what I looked like. I only had eyes for Chaser.

The vampire had spent the ride from the *Halcyon* falling in and out of consciousness, the desiccation creeping up his broken limbs, clawing away at his life with painful accuracy. The magic binding him to the talisman was gone, and there was no coming back this time. If Chaser died, it was forever.

Everything we'd fought for, we'd gotten. King was dead, the ritual was stopped, Loretta was avenged, Marini was a distant memory, and now... Now Chaser had to decide if he wanted to live as a half-vampire, half-wolf hybrid.

I could see the turmoil in his eyes every time he opened them and my heart broke. We'd risked everything and this is what we'd got.

"Sloane?"

I lifted my head at the sound of Wren's voice.

"It's time," she said. "I'll begin the spell on your word."

I knelt beside Chaser and cupped his face in my trembling, bloodstained hand. "Hey."

He wet his lips, his breathing ragged.

"It's time," I murmured, smoothing his hair away from his forehead. "Have you decided?"

"Do it," he whispered. "I trust you."

"Are you sure?" We both knew there was no going back.

"I want... I want to live for me," he managed to say. "I want to know what it's like to be free."

I kissed him, my lips pressing softly against his. "I love you."

"Sloane," Wren urged, "we're out of time."

Standing, I gazed down at Chaser, who's glassy eyes had never left mine. "Then begin."

"I need your blood," the witch said, holding up a knife and a plastic water bottle. "It'll sting."

I held out my arm. "Do whatever you need to."

The blade slid through my flesh, but I barely felt it. Blood rushed out of the cut and trickled into the bottle, dripping in a steady stream until Wren was satisfied she had enough.

Holding my arm against Hopper's shirt, I stood back as she knelt over Chaser and dipped her finger into my blood. She drew a strange symbol on his forehead, murmuring under her breath, then cut open his shirt and drew another over his heart.

Ringer wrapped his arm around my shoulder, pulling me against him. His presence was comforting as we watched Wren perform the ritual, and I was glad they were all here. They understood what Chaser had done for them. He'd not only freed me from the tyranny of King, but them as well.

Wren chanted, speaking words I didn't understand. She held the bottle to Chaser's lips, urging him to drink. He was sluggish, the desiccation moving more rapidly now that magic was being poured into his body.

Then Wren stood, holding her arms towards the sky, her voice rising as she called on magic beyond our comprehension.

Chaser coughed, spitting blood, and I lunged forwards, but Ringer held me back.

"Wren's got this," he murmured. "It'll be okay."

I let out a soft moan as I watched the blood trickle from Chaser's mouth, his eyes wide as he stared at the sky. Then he roared in agony as his back broke, the sound of bones cracking echoed through the clearing. He rolled onto his side, breathing heavily as his shredded arm cracked.

"Sloane, look," Stewie whispered.

We watched as the sickly grey hue that'd been creeping up his limbs receded, the desiccation fading. His ruined arm began to heal even as his bones started to transform.

"He's turning," Bones said. "*It's working.*"

Wren stood back, lowering her arms. "It's done. The rest is up to him."

"What do you mean?" I demanded.

"Chaser is a hybrid now, but to complete the ritual, he has to turn...and come back."

There was nothing any of us could do but watch as Chaser lay on the ground, writhing as his bones shattered. A wolf was being created before our eyes in slow motion; each cry that tore from Chaser's lips felt like a knife in my heart.

I wanted to go to him, to hold his body as it tore apart, but the wolves held me back as tears streamed from my eyes. What if the spell had gone wrong and all this pain was for nothing? What if he was dying?

What had I done?

I sobbed as fur began to sprout over Chaser's skin, his wolf emerging in a chaotic twist of magic that we could taste in the air.

He pushed to his newly grown paws as the last of his human body merged with the animal, and his final cry of pain erupted into a throaty growl.

Chaser stood in the middle of the clearing, his fur as black as a moonless night, his eyes iridescent silver as they gazed at us.

For a moment, I didn't know what he was going to do—attack or submit—but he turned, leaping into the bush.

"Chaser!" I shouted. "*Chaser!*"

"Turn," Stewie said. "Turn and run with him. Call him back."

"The first time is always the hardest," Bones added. "I can't imagine what he's going through as a hybrid."

"No one does," Davis said. "He's the first."

"Go," Ringer said, letting me go. "Go find him."

The wolves all looked to me, and I nodded. "Wait here with Wren. If I need you, I'll call."

I turned and ran into the bush, following Chaser's trail. The moment I was out of sight, I shifted, my body twisting into the wolf within. It was becoming less painful—the abrupt turning did a lot to help matters—though that was the last thing I was thinking about tonight.

All I could focus on was Chaser.

Even though my blood made him, he wasn't bound to the pack. I wasn't his alpha. Love would be the only thing that called to him now.

I caught his scent—a strange mixture of vampire and wolf—and followed his tracks through the trees.

I stopped where the trail was the strongest, my ears flicking as I listened to the sounds of the bush. The rustle of a mouse, the drone of a car in the distance, the clamouring of humans on the neighbouring property, and the determined footsteps of a predator.

Chaser leapt out of the darkness like a silent shadow, and we collided, rolling over and over in a mess of fur and teeth.

His wolf was in control, wrestling with his vampire instincts and at war with his humanity. What he needed now was someone to show him the way back to himself—the way to his soul. It lay on the other side of the battle, beyond the trauma of his past, the pain of his present, and the instincts born inside him. Every part of what made him was at odds with each other.

But I was in control. I knew who I was and now I knew the truth of what lay within Chaser's heart.

I could call him back.

Our tumbling slowed and I pushed with all my strength. Chaser's movements were sloppy, his wolf unsteady on its feet, and I came out on top. *Literally*.

I clamped my jaws around his neck, pressing just hard enough to assert my dominance.

I'm here, I pleaded, hoping he'd hear. *It's Sloane. Come back to me, Chaser. Come back.*

He growled, snapping and jerking underneath me.

I know who you are. I know the man under all that pain, under all that confusion. My jaws tightened as he struggled. *You're William Mason. You're fierce, strong, intelligent, and good. You love me and I love you. Freedom, love, forever.*

Recognition seemed to flood his eyes and his struggling stopped. I didn't know what had shifted inside him, but I knew I could let go. He wouldn't hurt me.

I stepped back and the black wolf stumbled to his paws, his head lowered.

His spine snapped, forcing his back upwards, then his legs followed. Chaser turned, his body twisting and growing. The agony and confusion he felt was clear in his eyes as each bone broke and realigned, his jaw cracking and his knees buckling.

When Chaser finally knelt before me as a man, he let out a moan and collapsed. He lay naked on the rough earth, his eyes closed, and didn't move.

The ritual was complete.

I stood over him and licked his face, but he didn't wake. Chaser was out cold, his body healed, his arm whole, but his mind... I didn't know who I'd meet when he woke up.

If he woke up, a small voice nagged.

Lifting my head, I howled, calling to the pack. *Come find me. Come find us.*

It was time to go home.

———

I closed the door behind me and sighed. Chaser still hadn't woken, his sleep so deep he couldn't be roused, not even by Wren.

She said he needed time. His body had been through a great deal of trauma, and he'd wake when he was ready and not a moment before.

Muffled sounds reverberated through the compound, but they barely registered. My mind was full of blood, death, and the ritual. Running through the bush with Chaser was... It'd taken my breath away.

It didn't feel right, standing here without him. I'd been alone for so long I'd gotten used to my own company, making my own decisions, doing my own thing. Now...I didn't know how I coped without him.

Most of all, I hoped he didn't regret choosing the ritual.

"Sloane?"

I turned, my heart beating double-time as I caught sight of a familiar form.

"Gasket!" I rushed forwards, and the old wolf wrapped his arms around me. He smelled the same, like oil and spice. Familiar.

"I'm so glad you're okay," he murmured.

"Are you okay? The pack?"

"We're good. Spike got run over."

I pulled back. "He got run over?"

"By a big-arse Harley," Gasket confirmed with a nod.

My bottom lip began to tremble.

"He's gonna be okay," he said, looking perplexed. "No one died."

"They didn't?"

Gasket shook his head and relief washed over me. "It was bedlam," he went on. "The whole place erupted. There was no way Rocket was going to surrender without a fight, but when we turned… Shit, Sloane, when we turned, it was…" His eyes sparkled with something that looked a lot like euphoria. "I had no idea. After a lifetime of turning on the full moon, of not remembering, it was…"

I raised an eyebrow. "Like being high?"

"This was better than drugs." He placed a fatherly hand on my leg. "Half the renegades submitted on the spot; the other half stood ground and fought."

"Rocket?"

Gasket's smile faded. "There was no submission for him. He's in the ground now, girl. Don't you worry about him."

I leaned back and sighed. After last night, there was a lot of supernaturals 'in the ground'. It was a damn shame it had come to this.

Gasket scratched his beard and sighed. "Listen, the guys... They want to know how you are."

"I'm okay. Physically, at least." My gaze shifted to the door.

Gasket's hand grasped my shoulder and gave a reassuring squeeze. "He's going to be okay, kid. I know it."

"I did it, Gasket," I said, my voice wavering. "We were caught... Then he separated us. King..." I sniffed and gathered my composure. "They were beating Chaser in the next room while King... They started the ritual. Gasket, if I hadn't escaped... We were so close to losing everything." I glanced at the door. "I still might lose him."

Gasket followed my gaze and nodded. "You don't have to tell me the details, Sloane. I get it. But you're here now, and he's gunna wake up. I have faith in Wren, she said the ritual went flawlessly."

We sat in silence, listening to the workings of the compound around us.

"God..." I said, thinking back to the moment I'd held Chaser in my arms at the *Halcyon*. The mayhem crew had stared down at me in horror, their expressions stabbing through my heart. "The looks on their faces when they found us."

"Don't focus on that," Gasket said. "They understand. You're not just their alpha, Sloane."

"Yeah?"

"They love you like a sister, like family."

It was what I'd always wanted. To be a part of something special. *To belong.*

"Gasket, I—" I took a deep breath. "What now? What do we do now? I need something to focus on, because if I stand here and dwell on everything, I..." I looked back at the door. Maybe I should be in there. Maybe I should wait by Chaser's side until he woke, but what about the pack? I was the alpha.

"We'll clean the place up and get the garage running again," Gasket told me. "In time, the city will be free from the last of the Hollow Men, and we'll be able to bring everyone back together. When you return, we'll decide what direction to take the pack in." He placed his big hand on my shoulder. "I'm only the caretaker, kid. You're the one they look up to."

I blinked. "When I return?"

"When Chaser wakes, I reckon you both need a holiday." His smile widened. "I hear Perth is nice this time of year."

I rubbed my hands up and down my arms. "Gasket... I-I'm afraid he won't wake up."

"You're scared you made the wrong decision?"

I nodded.

"The boys told me you gave him a choice."

"Yeah, but I—"

"But nothing, girl," he said. "Chaser's a grown man. He knew what he was getting into. You don't go holding that burden on your shoulders, you hear?"

I swallowed a fresh wave of tears and nodded.

The old wolf sighed, his eyes softening. "From what I hear, he was in bad shape. The spell might have healed him, but something like that takes time for the mind to reconcile. Magic does a great job of tricking our bodies, but our brains are too smart for it, girl." He wrapped his big arms around me. "He's gunna wake up. How could he not when he's got you waiting for him?"

"Freedom, love, forever," I whispered, pressing my cheek against his chest.

"Those things sound good to me," Gasket replied. "Bloody damn good."

CHAPTER 28
SLOANE

I took my helmet off and let the wind stream through my hair as I rode my motorcycle down the highway into the outer suburbs of Perth, Western Australia.

Life was like that these days. Grasping it whenever I could, relishing the reminders that I was alive. Speed, adrenaline, experience. It was the kind of living on the edge of danger that didn't include imminent death, and I liked it. *A whole lot.*

Behind me, I heard the roar of a second motorcycle over the road noise and smiled. Hitting the accelerator, I took the next exit and descended into the urban sprawl. Far in the distance, I could see the faint outline of the Perth skyline, and overhead, a few airplanes streaked across the clear blue sky.

Finally, after our epic cross-country road trip— which had been a much happier part two—I came to a stop outside a familiar apartment complex. The engines turned off, and the silence was almost deafening after the constant roar.

Chaser threw his leg over his bike and stood beside it. Ever since that night in the bush, he'd been different. His transformation had been hard on him—it'd taken three days for him to wake—and adjusting to his new reality wasn't easy. Many of his vampire traits had merged with his wolf, making his bloodlust rise to new levels. Chaser was a master of concealing his emotions, and if he struggled with any of it, he'd never told me.

While my story was coming to a close, his journey as the world's only hybrid was just beginning.

As I got off my motorcycle—my beautiful, black and blue Harley Speedster, custom painted by Gasket—my phone beeped. I reached into the inside pocket of my leather jacket, pulled it out, and pressed the button on the side. No more burner phone, either. I was now a certified adult with a phone bill...with my legal name on it, Sloane Mason. Chaser and I weren't married, not in the human sense, but I was getting the paperwork out of the way, or so I liked to say when I teased him. Marriage didn't matter, but there was no way I was going back to being a Marini, so Mason it was.

Staring at the message on the screen, I smiled.

"It's a text from Gasket," I said.

"Yeah? What's it say?"

I grinned and ran my fingers over the screen. "The garage is up and running again. Grand opening is tomorrow. He says I can pick up my apprenticeship anytime I want."

Chaser made a face and took my phone from me. "You? A mechanic?"

"Maybe I should go into private security."

"Somehow I think fixing up engines might be safer." Chaser flung his arm over my shoulder and hugged me against his side. "I love you."

"Huh? I can't hear you."

"I said, I love you."

I sighed contentedly.

"You heard me the first time, didn't you?"

"Yep. I just like hearing you say it."

He raised an eyebrow. "You know, people usually say it back."

"I love you, Chaser."

He smiled and nodded towards the building. "Have you decided what you're going to tell her?"

Should I tell Yvette the truth about me and the supernatural world? I'd thought about it non-stop from the moment we'd left Melbourne. The dilemma had plagued me right across the Nullarbor, percolated underneath the starry skies, and churned in the pit of my stomach as we approached Perth.

But in the end, I knew there wasn't a choice to be made.

"I think it's safer for her and her daughter if she doesn't know," I murmured.

It hurt to keep the truth from Yvette, especially after all the kindness she'd shown me, but I knew it was for the best. Even though the Hollow Men had all but disbanded, there were plenty of other dangers out there for a pack like Fortitude. As alpha, I would bear the brunt of it because it was my abilities that gave the wolves their freedom from the moon. Jealousy was just another predator on an already long list and would come knocking sooner rather than later.

Chaser nodded as if he'd already known and took my hand. "You wanna go up?"

"Yeah. Let's go."

We went upstairs, hand-in-hand, my body zinging with excitement. Standing in front of apartment fourteen, I danced from foot to foot and knocked on the door. They were going to flip. We hadn't called or texted—which would've seriously ruined the surprise.

The door opened, revealing a tall, leggy blonde and utter chaos behind her. Brittany was laughing up a storm, and over my friend's shoulder, I could see Sam on the floor, playing a lively game of Barbie dolls with the toddler.

"Sloane?" Yvette's mouth dropped open.

I grinned and threw my arms around her neck, holding her tight.

"You're here?" she asked. "You're really here?"

"As real as real can be."

She pulled back and ran her hands over my cheeks, then settled her palms on my shoulders.

I grinned, liking this forever feeling. Love, family, forever—the combination of Chaser's mantra and mine.

"How..." Yvette began.

"It's a long story, but I made you a promise...and I've been known to go to great lengths to keep them."

"I can't believe you're here!" She glanced at Chaser, her eyes narrowing slightly. "And *you*."

"I see I made quite the impression," the hybrid drawled. "Can I come in?"

Sighing, Yvette rolled her eyes. "Yeah, come on in." She waved us forwards, and Sam rose to greet us.

I grasped Chaser's hand, and we stepped into the apartment, across the threshold, and into the part that came after the struggle.

Into our forever.

**Want more novels just like this one? Check out
Nicole's other series:**

AUSTRALIAN SUPERNATURAL - In the harsh and
unforgiving Australian Outback lies the tiny opal
mining town of Solace. A witch runs the general store,
a vampire cuts and polishes opal, the mechanic is a
werewolf, a fae is the local layabout, and an elemental
works the mine. But what's hidden underneath the
baked earth is the most dangerous thing of all.

THE ARONDIGHT CODEX - An ancient war with
demons. A lost sword with the power to end it all. And
a woman with purple hair is the world's only hope.

THE CAMELOT ARCHIVE - Set in the same alternate
Arthurian world seen in **The Arondight Codex**...
Deadly secrets. Murder and revenge. The end of the
world is nye and Camelot is the last bastion of hope.

THE WITCH HUNTER SAGA - Vampires and witches
collide in this thrilling Urban Fantasy adventure.
You've never met vampires quite like these...

THE CRESCENT WITCH CHRONICLES - Witches,
shapeshifters, and ancient myth collide in this
colourful Irish flavoured series! Come on an adventure

fraught with danger and forbidden romance... and the ultimate battle to save magic before it's gone forever.

THE DARKLAND DRUIDS - A woman with no living relatives travels from Australia to the other side of the world to find out the truth of who she is...only to land in the middle of a prophecy of destruction. Druids, witches, fae, and shapeshifters abound in this thrilling magical adventure!

Find out more at: NicoleRTaylorWrites.com

See what titles are FREE at: Nicole's Free Reads

ABOUT NICOLE

Nicole R. Taylor is an Australian Urban Fantasy author.

She lives in the western suburbs of Melbourne dreaming up nail biting stories featuring sassy witches, duplicitous vampires, hunky shapeshifters, and devious monsters.

She likes chocolate, cat memes, and video games.

When she's not writing, she likes to think of what she's writing next.

Follow Nicole Online:

Website: nicolertaylorwrites.com
Facebook: facebook.com/nrtaylorwrites
Newsletter: nicolertaylorwrites.com/newsletter

www.ingramcontent.com/pod-product-compliance
Lightning Source LLC
Chambersburg PA
CBHW060815190726
48285CB00002B/671